Dee

"Books ca. ~~~~ ?"

(abbe)

"I hope this   exception!"

(Mike Redmond)

9: IV: 01

Settling the Score

Settling the Score

MIKE REDMOND

A Black Horse Western

ROBERT HALE · LONDON

© Mike Redmond 2000
First published in Great Britain 2000

ISBN 0 7090 6681 3

Robert Hale Limited
Clerkenwell House
Clerkenwell Green
London EC1R 0HT

Typeset by
Derek Doyle & Associates, Liverpool.
Printed and bound in Great Britain by
WBC Book Manufacturers Limited, Bridgend.

ONE

As the northbound stage drew up outside the telegraph office in a swirl of dust, the shotgun rider jumped down before the wheels had even stopped turning. That was all there was to it most days: mail in, mail out. Any passengers generally sat tight, headed for the railroad at Madson's Crossing. This afternoon was different though.

The driver climbed down, walked around and held open the door.

'Three Rocks, mister – and welcome to it.'

A young man stepped out, planted his feet firmly on the ground and stretched his cramped limbs with the air of someone more at ease in the saddle than inside a stage. The trail this afternoon had evidently been hot and bumpy. Meanwhile the shotgun had already emerged from the office with a bag of mail and was climbing back aboard.

'This yours, mister?'

He pointed to a saddle roll lodged against the roof rack.

'Reckon so.'

The roll descended without ceremony into its owner's outstretched arms. Then the driver whistled up the horses and the stage rattled off. As the new arrival stood by one of the hitching rails, looking round uncertainly, a voice

5

from the shadows of the porch outside the telegraph office rasped, 'Why don't you come up here, mister? Kind of hot just standing there in the sun.'

The stranger shrugged, shouldered his saddle roll, and stepped up into the shade. An old-timer was sitting on a bench with his hat half tilted over his eyes.

'You work here?'

'Nope. I just sit here. Don't get much activity in this town. But what we do get, we mostly get here or down aways at the saloon.'

The stranger grimaced. There were a few horses hitched along the way, and inside the office he could hear the spasmodic chattering of the telegraph, but apart from that the old man seemed to be the only sign of life. His instinct told him to find a mount, ride on out and finish the last leg of his journey. But it had been a long day and he wasn't inclined to face the best part of a seven-mile ride near sundown on a trail he scarcely remembered.

'Anywhere I can get a room for the night?'

'Try Ma Blaney's, couple of blocks down. Name's over the door. You should be all right. She don't get much passing trade in a place like this.'

The old-timer guffawed and shook his head at his own wit.

'Thanks.'

The stranger walked off slowly, his boots echoing on the wooden boards in the silence of the afternoon. He reached the house and tried the door. Finding it unlocked he rapped once with his free hand and let himself inside.

'Something I can do for you, mister?'

A woman aged about forty, dressed in black, was standing at the back of a small, gloomy lobby studying a ledger on the counter beside her. The stranger took off his hat.

'Afternoon, ma'am. I was told you might be able to let me have a room for the night.'

'Reckon I might – always assuming you can pay up front. No offence intended, but that's the way of it here.'

He walked across, produced some greenbacks from his pocket and dropped them on the counter.

'That enough?'

'Oh, sure, mister. This ain't no fancy dude hotel. Just one night, you said?' There was a tinge of regret in her voice.

'That's right, ma'am.'

'Care to sign the book, then?' She indicated the next empty line in the ledger. 'Don't make much difference to me whether you signs or not, but Sheriff Westlake likes it like that.'

'All right.'

The stranger took the pen she was offering, dipped it in the inkwell and signed his name in a clear bold hand.

'Thanks, Mr . . er. . . .'

'Sefton, ma'am – Hank Sefton.'

Ma Blaney studied him for a moment, just as she sized up anyone who walked through her door. He was travel-stained but his general appearance was reassuring. Beneath a shock of well-brushed light-brown hair his face, although shadowed by a day's stubble, had a regular clean-cut appearance, and his legs were a sight straighter than you usually saw with the local ranch hands. His shirt, under a neat leather vest, was well cut and reasonably clean. His pants seemed to have been pressed within recent memory and his boots showed quality under the dust.

'Perhaps you'd. . . .'

'Oh, sure. Sorry, young man, I'm forgetting my manners.' She reached behind the counter and handed him a key.

'First right, top of the stairs.'

An hour or so later a well-scrubbed and shaved Hank

Sefton stepped out of Ma Blaney's in search of liquor and entertainment. Not that there was much choice, as Ma Blaney had told him with total frankness when she poured his bath. You either went to the Nugget Saloon or you stayed in your room counting the cracks in the ceiling. He made his way stiffly along the sidewalk. The best part of a day in the stage had creased up his muscles, and his gunbelt felt uncomfortably lopsided. On the cattle drives up the Chisholm Trail he normally toted a six-shooter on each hip on the basis that you never could tell which side trouble was coming from. But tonight he'd nearly allowed himself the luxury of sashaying out with no gunbelt at all. Then caution had got the better of him: he didn't know the town or any of its characters. So he'd compromised – a gun by his right hand just in case.

He reached the saloon, pushed through the swing doors, walked over to the bar, and flung down a few coins.

'Whiskey. And keep it coming.'

'Yes, sir.'

The barman studied the money for a moment, and then poured him a shot of rye – leaving the bottle at his disposal. Evidently the stranger's credit was good for the contents.

'Just got in, mister?'

'Yup.'

Sefton downed the first shot and helped himself to a second. No doubt about it: whiskey was sure the fastest way to put the trail behind you.

'Been travelling far?'

'Yuma.'

'Guess that's far enough. Don't get many strangers in this one-horse town. You on business out here?'

'Kind of.'

'Sure thing.'

Sefton's tone had discouraged any further enquiry so

the barman made busy polishing some glasses. Sefton looked around without much enthusiasm. If the Nugget was all Three Rocks had to offer, the sooner he was out of here in the morning, the better. A few drifters were sprinkled around obviously waiting for someone to buy them a drink, and a cowhand was strumming tunelessly at a beaten-up old piano in the corner. Close by the bar at a green baize-covered table a poker game was in progress. Sefton sipped his second drink and watched the progress of the game closely.

'That the biggest game in town?'

There was a note of contempt in his voice as he addressed the barman, speaking loudly enough to be heard by the players at the table.

The barman leant over the bar and lowered his voice. 'Mister, that's the *only* game in town. Them's the Ellwood boys – Mike and Pat – with a few of Jack Ellwood's ranch hands from the Double L. Guess it's an easy way for Jack to get best part of his payroll back on a Friday night. His two boys just rake it in from the poor suckers. They should stick to the bunkhouse.'

'That so?' said Sefton, unimpressed. 'Don't seem much call to be losing out to that sort of talent.'

As he spoke, the cowhand at the piano chose exactly the same moment to stop strumming so that Sefton's words fell into the unexpected silence. One of the card players looked up.

'Something riling you, mister?'

Sefton shrugged, and turned back to the bar.

'I said, something riling you, mister?'

The aggression in the voice was unmistakable.

'Watch it, mister,' muttered the barman. 'That's Pat – and he don't take kindly to turned backs.'

Sefton faced the card players. 'Just wondering about the style of play, that's all.'

'Is that so? Then why don't you sit yourself down and show us how good you are?'

Sefton shrugged again. 'All right. What are you playing for?'

'Fifty cents ante, and five bucks maximum. Jacks or better to open. That too much for you?' There was a general jeer from around the table at this sally.

'Think I can manage it. Deal me in, then.'

Sefton left his bottle and glass on the bar. Liquor and poker didn't go together, leastways, not if you wanted to get up a winner. A few years on the range had taught him that – the hard way. He sat down and concentrated on the cards and his opponents. Real poor stuff just as he'd seen from the bar – and most of them sauced out of their minds. He bided his time and took his opportunities when they turned up. It never paid to try to hurry lady luck. After an hour or so, when he'd busted both the Ellwoods out of pots they thought they should have won, he was showing a tidy profit and the atmosphere around the baize was growing perceptibly frostier.

'Guess we got ourselves a real fancy player, for once,' said Pat Ellwood, glancing round the table at his father's employees. He scratched the side of his face slowly.

'Feel like raising the stakes, mister? As you're so good, that is. Least you can do is give us a chance to get our money back.'

Sefton nodded. 'OK by me.'

Ellwood turned to one of the other hands, who, Sefton had worked out through the conversation round the table, was the Ellwood Ranch foreman.

'Deal 'em, then, Chuck. Dollar ante, and ten bucks max.'

The game continued, but now Sefton didn't much take to the way some of the pots were turning out. Especially when Chuck was dealing. The pile of notes and silver in front of Sefton drifted steadily downwards, just about in pace with the raising of his suspicions. Chuck was dealing again and Sefton was in the pot – a couple of aces to open with and three callers behind him, including Pat Ellwood. Sefton flicked his discards over to Chuck.

'I'll take three. . . .' His eyes narrowed as Chuck slid three cards towards him. 'And this time I'd be obliged to get them off the top of the deck, instead of the bottom.'

Sefton sat back and eyed the foreman calmly. There was a moment's silence and then Chuck exploded.

'Why you sassy, loud-mouthed son of a. . . . You calling me a cheat, mister?'

'Guess you could call it that,' smiled Sefton. 'Although not a very good one.'

With an oath, Chuck hurled the remainder of the deck of cards at Sefton's head, stumbled out of his chair and reached for his gun. But before any of the other card players could make a move Sefton had heaved the table over on to their laps, pinning them momentarily to their chairs under a cascade of notes and coins while he stood up and slicked his Colt out of its holster. Chuck's gun was only half drawn when there was an explosion of smoke and Sefton's first bullet clipped his right hand, sending the firearm spinning to the floor. As Chuck stood clutching at his wounded hand, Pat Ellwood extracted himself from underneath the table and signalled to the barman.

'Deal with him, Lou!'

Sefton glanced around and was just quick enough to prevent the whiskey bottle which had been standing on the bar from hitting him full over the head. Instead, it struck him a glancing blow on the cheek, knocking him sideways into the waiting arms of Mike Ellwood and one of the other ranch hands. Sefton struggled for a moment, but they had his arms pinioned behind his back, and he never believed in resisting superior odds.

Pat Ellwood walked round and faced Sefton, eyeball to eyeball.

'Guess you think it's smart to shoot up my pa's number-one hand. I don't know where you've come from, mister, but round these parts we don't take too kindly to trail skunks who go around bad mouthing folks when they're losing at cards. Maybe we'd better teach you some manners.'

He nodded at Sefton's captors who tightened their grip on his arms. Then he stood back a little and swung a vicious punch into Sefton's belly. As Sefton doubled up in agony, Ellwood drove a second into his face, knocking his head back against the shoulder of one of the men who was holding him.

'Keep him upright, boys,' said Ellwood. 'I'm just getting warmed up.'

He gathered himself to continue the punishment, but before he could draw his fist back, the swing doors behind Ellwood crashed open and a voice spoke calmly but sternly, 'That's enough boys. I'll take over from here.'

There was an immediate loosening of the tension in the atmosphere and the tightness with which Sefton was being held. His vision was a bit blurred from the impact of Ellwood's two punches, but as he raised his head he was able to make out a tall figure in black pants and vest standing behind Ellwood. The newcomer had a tin star pinned on his chest.

'Sure glad you're here, Matt,' mumbled Ellwood in tones that suggested otherwise. 'See what this palooka nearly done to Chuck here? Dang nearly shot his hand off. And we were only playing a friendly game of cards.'

'That right? Ain't that just too bad.'

The sheriff turned to Sefton. 'Wouldn't advise you to try any fancy gun play in Three Rocks, youngster. I've got my office plumb in the centre of town where I can hear everything. Didn't take but a moment to walk over here and size up the action.'

Sefton shook his head. 'That two-bit punk was cheating me, Sheriff. He was dealing off the bottom of the deck. I figure I've got the right to protect myself here as well as anywhere else.'

'Not with a six-shooter you haven't,' returned the sheriff. 'Leastways, not in my town.'

He reached in his back pocket and produced a pair of handcuffs.

'I'm taking you in, mister.'

'Come on, Sheriff,' protested Sefton, 'they were cheating me. Ain't there no justice in this town?'

'Sure is . . .' said the sheriff, drawing Sefton's reluctant hands out from behind his back and fastening them with the cuffs. 'And you're looking at it.'

The sheriff turned to the Ellwoods and their henchmen. 'All right, boys. Fun's over. Back to your game. Looks like I got me a guest for the night.'

'The hell you have, Matt,' protested Chuck, wrapping a kerchief around his wounded hand. 'The two-bit little skunk just shot up my gun hand. Why don't you just leave him to us? Ain't no call to be cluttering up the jail with this trail trash, when we can string him up outside.'

The sheriff looked sceptically at Chuck's injury but showed no inclination to let go of his prisoner. 'Too bad about the hand, Chuck. Maybe you'll have to try dealing left handed.'

Putting a firm hand on Sefton's shoulder the sheriff pushed him out through the saloon doors and along the boardwalk – Sefton protesting his innocence all the way. A couple of blocks along they came to a lighted window beside a glass-paned door bearing the stencilled inscription *Matthew Westlake, Sheriff, Three Rocks*.

The sheriff's office was a sparsely furnished room with

a desk, a firearms cabinet, a filing chest and, at the back, an iron grille giving on to what looked like the one and only cell. Westlake kept his grip on Sefton's shoulder until he had swung open the grille. Then he unbuckled Sefton's gunbelt and thrust him inside. He closed the grille, locked it with a key produced from a bunch hanging up on the wall alongside and sat back on the edge of his desk to contemplate his prisoner.

'You're making a big mistake, Sheriff. I swear they were cheating me. You've got no call to keep me under lock and key. I tell you I was only protecting myself. And you've no right to keep me trussed up like a turkey in these cuffs. Is this what counts for justice around here?'

'Son, you sure sound off big. Do you ever let anyone else get a word in?'

'Depends on who it is, I guess. I just don't like being arrested when I've done nothing wrong. It never happened to me till I came here.'

Westlake shook his head. 'Who said anything about being arrested?'

Sefton looked down disbelievingly at the handcuffs, and rattled the bars of the cell.

'What do you call this, then – a cruise up the Mississippi?'

'Don't get smart with me son. Let's say I prefer to call it protection.'

'I'm not being smart with you, Sheriff. All I'm saying is, I know enough about cards to be sure when someone's cheating me.'

'That so? Well, maybe that Chuck was cheating you, but if you were smart enough to spot it why weren't you smart enough to pick up your cash and walk away? They outnumbered you – or didn't you notice?'

Sefton hung his head. 'Maybe.'

Westlake stood up and approached the grille. 'Son, you

got a choice. You can spend the night in there shackled and railing against injustice, or you can calm down and talk reasonable with your hands free. I already told you you're not under arrest. Which do you want?'

Sefton considered. 'I'll talk reasonable if you'll take these cuffs off.'

He thrust his hands up against the bars. Westlake produced a small key and unlocked the handcuffs.

'Right, now sit down on that bunk and act quiet.'

Sefton glanced behind him and saw that there was a wooden-framed bunk with a dirty straw-filled palliasse on top. He sat down gingerly on the edge.

'Good,' said Westlake. 'Let's get down to formalities. What's your name?'

'Sefton, Hank Sefton.'

'How old are you?'

'Twenty-three.'

'You got business in town? I knows you only stepped off the stage this afternoon.'

'Sort of. Leastways, I've got a reason for being here.'

'Such as?'

Sefton stood up, fumbled in the back pocket of his denims, and produced a creased letter which he handed through the grille to Westlake.

The sheriff read the paper and handed it back. 'All right. You fixing to be around here long?'

With a shrug Sefton answered with a question of his own. 'Sheriff, what did you mean just now by protection? I can look after myself.'

'Oh sure. You were doing a real fine job of it when I walked in. The Ellwoods would have beaten you to a pulp and left you out in the desert as coyote fodder. Have you got any idea who they are? Old man Ellwood owns half the county and he won't take kindly to finding his foreman's had his hand blistered by one of your bullets.'

'That was an accident – I was aiming for his gun, not his hand.'

'Whatever. The Ellwoods won't read it that way. This is the safest place in town for you till they cool down.'

'So how long's that going to be?'

Westlake made no immediate reply, but pulled out a bentwood armchair from behind his desk, set it in front of the grille, propped his feet up on one of the horizontal bars and made himself comfortable. Sefton looked a sight more intelligent than most of the company generally available in Three Rocks, business was quiet apart from a worrying message that had come over the wire this morning, and he had nobody else to talk to.

'Well, let's take it easy shall we? Come midnight them Ellwoods should be so stewed with liquor they'll need to be tied on to their horses to make it back to their spread. That's the usual way it is on Friday nights. You'll be safe enough, then. In the meantime . . . . why, we might even try a hand or two of cards. You can trust me . . . I'm the sheriff.'

TWO

About the same time that Hank Sefton was stepping off the stage in Three Rocks, two riders approached the shade of a couple of high boulders at the rim of a range of bluffs some miles to the east and stared down at the farmstead below.

'Can't see nobody but the woman.'

The older of the two men tilted his hat a little more over his eyes to shield out the glare from the late afternoon sun and gave the spread a final survey. A one-storey log house with a few outbuildings, a corral with a couple of mounts, and an arroyo running alongside the track that they figured led into Salto Creek – all just as quiet as they needed it. He swivelled in his saddle, jutting his unshaven chin towards his companion.

'You thinking what I'm thinking, Brother?'

The other rider completed his own survey and nodded his head.

'Looks just right, Abe. Guess we ain't got much choice anyway. These mounts won't go much further 'less we get them fed and watered. And this leg doesn't need any more saddle work.'

He gestured down to his left thigh where a blood-stained bandanna was just visible inside his chap.

Abe eased his sidearms slightly out of their holsters so

17

as to be ready for the unexpected and set his horse into a walk, picking his way carefully down the escarpment towards the stream. His brother followed behind, wincing occasionally as his horse paced unevenly over the scree giving his damaged leg the odd painful jolt against the stirrup. They kept their eyes fixed on the farmstead. The woman had set herself to gathering and folding some clothes that had been drying on a washing line that stretched from the side of the farmhouse towards the clapboard privy. There was a curl of blue smoke from the farmhouse chimney and, as they got closer, they could smell the log fire that was presumably flickering in the hearth inside. That was a welcome prospect too. They'd sweated hell out there on the trail during the day, but the nights turned cold enough come sundown.

The horses quickened their pace a little as the path evened out and they approached the wooden fence that marked the frontage of the farmstead. The young man's horse, tired as his master and scenting the prospect of water and forage after a long hard day, nickered softly in anticipation. Until now, their careful approach had not been observed. The woman had her back to them and was intent on her work. Abe noted with satisfaction that, at least from the rear, she looked as good a handful as any man had a right to expect after a hard day's ride. Pretty, braided blonde hair, and a trim figure in a pale-blue dress.

As the horse's nicker caught her attention she turned round from the clothes line. For a moment she stood still – one hand on the line, the other on her hip, sizing them up. Salto Creek was a thinly populated little neighbourhood where folks all knew each other and where you didn't get many strangers passing through. She was evidently waiting see whether they were intending to ride on, but when they turned their horses into the open gate she left her laundry line and walked across the dusty yard towards them. Abe pulled in his horse, but did not dismount. Now they were closer to the house he could hear the sound of someone chopping wood behind the barn that stood a little way to one side. Before committing himself he wanted to see who the other person was. He raised his hat as the woman approached.

'Afternoon, ma'am. Guess it's a pretty darn hot one.'

'That's the way of it out here.'

Her voice was neutral, conveying no particular hint of welcome, and her face registered wariness at the two men's appearance. The younger man in particular was visibly holding himself very stiffly in his saddle, his knuckles clenched white around the pommel.

Abe hesitated. The woman's tone of voice was discouraging and there was that unseen somebody behind the barn. He noted that she was wearing a wedding ring. Close up he could see that she was really good-looking. Not made up, or anything fancy, but nice lively blue eyes that went well with her frock, and a pretty little mouth. Abe reckoned she must be rising thirty but the heat and toil that went with life out here in the Southwest didn't seem to have worked its way into her face the way it mostly did with range women. He wrenched his thoughts away from her and concentrated on the problem at hand. He was about to speak again when the sound of wood chopping stopped and a boy of about twelve or thirteen emerged from behind the barn with firewood under each arm. He checked his pace when he saw the two riders and then walked warily up to them.

'That your boy, ma'am?'

'Sure is.'

'Guess he must be. Sure takes after his ma in looks.'

The boy had his mother's blue eyes and regular features under a thatch of corn-blond hair.

'Ma'am, my name's Abe Lancing and this is my pardner

Seth. Guess we're just about all in after a day on the trail. Same goes for the horses. You got anywheres we could lay up quiet for the night? We wouldn't give you no trouble and we can pay for the fodder.' He fished in his shirt pocket and produced a couple of silver coins.

'Don't see why not.'

Her voice was still reluctant, but cash was cash and there wasn't much of it around these parts. Besides, whatever he looked like, Abe had asked politely enough and it was difficult to refuse hospitality.

'Guess you can bunk down in the barn comfortable enough. There's plenty of straw. And Patch'll take care of your horses real good.'

Lancing raised his hat again, nodded at his brother and dismounted, hefting off the saddle pouches and slinging them over his shoulder.

'Much obliged to you, ma'am.'

He led his horse forward a little way towards the boy, carefully cutting off the woman's view of his brother as he lifted himself painfully out of his saddle.

'Here you are, Patch,' said Abe, setting the horses' heads towards the boy. 'Sure appreciate your trouble.'

The woman's features relaxed slightly and she permitted herself a dry chuckle.

'That's not Patch, mister. My boy's called Cal and I'm Wilma. Wilma Riley.' Before Abe could say anything she turned towards the barn and shouted, 'Patch! Patch! You just stir your hide and get on out here. There's work to be done. Can't stay lazing inside all afternoon. You hear me?'

A shadow appeared at the barn door and a wizened Indian, barefoot and dressed in leggings with a red check shirt limped his way towards them.

'Now this, this is Patch,' said Wilma Riley. 'Not much of a name – short for Apache, of course – but then he ain't much of an Indian. Game in one leg and only half a brain, but he's real good with horses. Kind of hard to find much help in these parts so you takes what you can get.'

As the Indian came up to them she gestured towards the horses. 'See to 'em, Patch.'

The Indian made no sound but collected the bridles and prepared to lead the horses off.

'Just a moment, ma'am,' said Abe hurriedly. He turned back to his saddle and extracted the Springfield that was holstered alongside the cinch strap.

'No offence, ma'am. But I don't take no chances with Injuns – even dumb ones. Specially dumb ones. Reckon this is best kept sleeping alongside me.'

'Suit yourself, mister.'

Wilma Riley's countenance still registered uncertainty and suspicion. If she had felt a bit more confident about these two she might have invited them into the farmhouse, but something didn't seem quite right. Especially about the way the one called Seth was holding himself. Nor was his face the type to reassure her with its shifty, watery blue eyes, a weak chin and a protruding upper lip scarcely concealed by a wispy blond moustache.

'Well, you go right along to the barn and make yourselves comfortable. Guess you wouldn't say no to some coffee and cornmeal cakes.'

'Why, no, ma'am. If it's not too much trouble for you.'

'No trouble. Coffee's on stove anyway. I'll get Cal to fetch it over for you.'

Abe and Seth stood motionless until the woman and her son had disappeared inside. Then they made their way towards the barn. Seth was limping heavily as the circulation came back to his legs. A curtain at the window of the farmhouse twitched slightly as Wilma Riley, still cautious, surveyed their progress across the farmyard. She turned to Cal who had put down the firewood at the side of the hearth and was standing beside her.

'Can't say as I like the looks of either of them two, specially with your father being over in Three Rocks until tomorrow fetching those supplies. And he's taken the shotgun, of course. Here boy. . . .' She lifted the enamel coffee pot off the stove, thrust it in Cal's left hand, and a couple of wooden beakers in his right. He winced.

'Hey, Ma, that's sure burning my hand.'

'Land sakes! Get on over with it, Cal. And you keep your ears open, mind. Like as not they won't be so careful what they say in front of a kid. I sure would really like to know what they've been up to.'

Cal grinned. Nothing much happened around here one day to another, and life had seemed quiet since his younger brother Amos had stepped on that rattler a couple of years back and hadn't made it through the night. Now, with his father gone over to Three Rocks, he was ready to seize the opportunity to play the man of the house. He made his way over to the barn and peered inside. Seth was lying full length on a pile of straw with the saddle pouches under his head as a cushion, while his brother was propped up on an old trestle table that Jess Riley used for cutting the heads off chickens when they were pot bound. Abe sniffed appreciatively as the aroma of freshly brewed coffee filled the barn.

'Well done, boy. Set it down here.'

Cal put the coffee pot and beakers down on the table beside Abe and stood back cautiously. Abe poured coffee into the two beakers and held one out to the boy.

'Here. Give this to my brother. Guess he's fair whacked out with all the riding we've done since sun-up.'

Cal took the coffee, crouched down, and passed it to Seth. Then he stood up and looked around uncertainly. His mother had told him to keep his ears open, but neither of the two men seemed inclined to say anything. Seth took a swig at his coffee and groaned.

'I sure needed that.' He sat up and stared at the boy.
'Can you get me some hot water, boy? I really need to get
the trail dust off my hide.'

'Sure, mister.'

Cal ran back to the house where his mother was still
standing at the window eyeing the barn door.

'Ma, they's asking for some hot water. All right if I take
over the kettle?'

'Ain't the trough good enough for them to duck their
heads? Oh well, guess there's no harm in keeping them
happy.'

The kettle was heavy copper and pretty near full, but
Cal made a good job of lifting it off the iron range and
carrying it across the stone floor without slopping any of
the water. He made his way back to the barn and set the
kettle down. The two men were still in the positions he'd
left them in.

'There's a bucket yonder, mister,' he said, pointing to a
corner by the table.

'All right.'

Abe stood up and grunted irritably as Cal remained
staring inquisitively at them with his pale-blue eyes.

'Ain't no call for you to be hanging around us, boy. We
got all we need. You just skedaddle.'

Cal backed out as Abe kicked the barn door shut
behind him. That suited him just fine for his next move.
Instead of going back to the house he walked round the
side of the barn and slipped off his boots. At the far end a
ladder was propped up against the wooden wall reaching
as far as the open entrance to the barn loft. Taking care to
make no sound he climbed carefully up the ladder and
wriggled his way into the loft.

'Just get your britches down and let's have a look-see at
that wound,' said Abe, putting down his empty coffee
mug.

Seth unbuckled his two belts and manoeuvred his pants down to reveal a bloodstained thigh. He yelped as Abe soaked a kerchief in the hot water he'd poured in the bucket and applied it to the open wound.

'No call to be hissing like a scalded tom cat. You've had worse than this.'

'Maybe I have, but it still hurts like tarnation. How bad is it?'

'There's a hole in and a hole out. You were lucky.'

Abe concentrated on the business of cleaning up. The damage wasn't that bad provided Seth could keep the wound clean and properly bandaged. In the sudden silence a creaking sound from somewhere in the barn caught his attention.

'What was that?'

They stared around but the daylight was fading and the far corners of the barn were filled with shadows.

'Rats, I guess,' said Abe.

He levered himself up from beside his brother and walked to the door.

'Where you going?'

'That wound needs cauterizing. Best thing is if I splash some alcohol on it. We've still got some of that gut-busting aguardiente in one of the canteens.'

Abe went outside and walked over to the corral where the two horses had their noses in a bowl of mash. The saddles had been draped over the top rail of the fencing, but when Abe examined his own, the canteen was nowhere to be seen.

'Tarnation,' he muttered to himself. 'Them Apaches can smell out liquor at a hundred mile.'

He looked around but there was no sign of the Indian. To one side of the corral was a shed which looked as though it might be in use as a tackle store. The door was open. Abe walked across silently as a cat and positioned himself so that he could peer in the doorway. The Apache was standing with his back to him. He had unscrewed the stopper of the canteen and had lifted it up to sniff cautiously at the contents.

'You goddam thievin' varmint,' snarled Abe.

He launched a vicious kick with the tip of his pointed boot into the Indian's rump sending him staggering across the shed, while the canteen dropped to the wooden floor. The Indian recovered his balance and swung round to face him, his right hand going to his belt where there was a knife tucked inside a leather sheath. He never got a chance to use it. Abe closed right in on him and jerked his knee hard up into his groin. As the Indian folded up with a grunt Abe landed a sledge-hammer punch on his jaw knocking him backwards flat out on the floor.

'You got me really riled up, Injun!'

Before the Apache could make any further move, Abe had pounced on him, drawn the knife from its sheath and plunged it clean as a whistle between the ribs on the left side of the Indian's chest. Patch groaned, drummed his heels on the floor, twitched just once and lay still as Abe gave the knife a final unnecessary twist.

'Only good Injun's a dead'n,' muttered Abe to himself with satisfaction as he stood up, collected the canteen and shook it. Still a good slug of liquor inside, by the sound of it. He allowed himself a generous swig and then screwed the stopper back on. The rest was for his brother's wound.

As Abe re-entered the barn and crouched beside his brother Cal wriggled himself with extreme caution towards the edge of the loft gallery. He watched as Abe trickled the contents of his canteen over the wound in Seth's exposed thigh.

'Moses!' gasped Seth. 'That stuff packs a mule's kick outside or in.'

He lay back as Abe finished the medical treatment and made a fair go of tying a decent bandage.

'Guess you can pull them britches up now. We best get some sleep.'

Seth fastened his belt. Then he reached up, unbuckled one of the pouches, drew out a fistful of banknotes, and let them cascade on to the straw.

'How about these for a mighty nice pillow, Brother?' he chuckled. 'I never slept on three grand before!'

The sight of so much money was making Cal's eyes pop from his vantage point in the loft. Anxious to miss nothing he attempted to inch himself closer to the edge of the platform. In doing so his hand disturbed the layer of dust and hay seeds which lay thick over every surface inside the barn. The next moment the timbers echoed to the sound of the sneeze which he had been unable to stifle as the dust got up his nose.

'What in tarnation . . . that sure ain't no rat.'

Abe looked up and even in the gathering gloom he had no difficulty in spotting Cal's mop of fair hair. Before the boy could make any move his six-shooter was in his hand and pointing menacingly upward. 'You get down here right now, boy. No monkey business or I'll blow your goddamned brains out.'

Cal stood up reluctantly and climbed down to the two men.

'Looks like we got a real little smart-pants,' remarked Abe, as his brother stood up and brushed himself down.

'Sure do,' said Seth.

He reached forward and pulled Cal towards him by the front of his shirt. Then he brought his hand down on the side of the boy's face, left and right and again, in four measured whacks. Cal yelled, sinking to his knees as a trickle of blood jetted from one of his nostrils.

'Please mister, I didn't mean no harm. I'm always playing in here. My pa says it's all right.'

'Ages since I laced a boy,' remarked Seth calmly to

nobody in particular. 'But I ain't forgotten how.'

He reached down, grasped a handful of Cal's hair and lifted the squirming boy to his feet.

'Now, you can give me some more practice or you can answer some questions real truthful. Which do you want?'

Cal wiped his sleeve across his nose and sniffed. 'Don't hit me again, mister. I'll tell you anything.'

'So you have got a pa?'

'Yes.'

'Where is he, then? We ain't seen no sign of him round here.'

'He took the buckboard over to Three Rocks for some supplies.'

'When's he due back? No lies now.'

This time it was Abe who raised his hand threateningly. Cal backed away slightly. His eyes were swivelling to right and left searching for a means of escape, but he could feel the edge of the table behind him blocking off any further retreat.

'Tomorrow morning, mister. That's the truth, I swear.'

'Anyone else here, apart from that Injun?'

'Nope.'

'That's all right then,' said Seth, easing himself back down on the floor. His wounded leg wasn't liking too much pressure at the moment.

'Guess we can really treat ourselves to some home comforts,' said Abe, staring down at his brother with a smirk.

As he took his eyes off Cal, the boy seized his opportunity. He grabbed the half-full coffee pot from the table and flung pot and its steaming contents full in Abe's face. Then he scuttled out of the barn and ran ducking and weaving back to the house.

THREE

The coffee had gone off the boil but it stung Abe's eyes.

'That goddam little sidewinder.'

Seth staggered to his feet as his brother brushed his sleeve across his face, blinking in helpless rage. A quick glance out the barn door showed them that the boy had calculated his chances really well. Already he was on the farmhouse stoop and reaching for the door. Seth unholstered his gun, but Abe put a restraining hand on his arm.

'Don't waste a bullet, Brother. This one needs some cool figuring.' He gestured with his head back into the barn.

'Knew I should've knocked his head off,' muttered Seth.

'Maybe you should. But it's sure too late now. Question is – how much does he know?'

Seth scratched his head. 'Well, I reckon he was up there right from the time he brung the water. That means he knows I'm wounded. Won't take long for his ma to figure out that we ain't a pair of visiting preachermen.'

'That's right. But she knew that anyway. I saw how she was looking at us. So what's she going to do about it? According to the boy her old man's over in town. So it's two against one.'

Seth looked doubtful as he figured the arithmetic.

'What about the Injun? Can't reckon him out of the picture even if he is a bean-brain.'

'Sure can if he's got a knife stuck through his ribs.' Abe chuckled at the look of surprise on his brother's face.

'You mean. . . ?'

'I mean he's gone to the happy hunting grounds. Caught the dirty rattlesnake pilfering our liquor, so I let him have it with his own knife.'

Seth breathed a sigh of relief as the odds seemed to have been restored in their favour. Then a look of puzzlement spread over his face. 'So what next?'

'Great Moses, boy, what happened to your face?'

Wilma Riley examined her son in consternation as he launched himself through the farmhouse door, slamming and barring it behind him. Red blotches had sprung up on both sides of his face where Seth had recently applied his hand, and a stream of blood had congealed under his nose.

'One of 'em whacked me, Ma – real hard. They caught me keyholing them in the barn.'

Cal buried his head in his mother's apron for a moment, and then evidently remembered that he was the man of the house with a report to make. He stood back abruptly.

'They're bad, Mom. I seen it for myself. One of them's wounded in his leg and they're carrying a mint of money in those saddle-bags.'

'That's all we need with your pa away. Here, let's clean you up.'

She dipped a cloth in a bucket of cold water that was standing by the stove and pressed it to the boy's swollen face. While she was applying the cloth her mind was racing as she tried to work out what to do next. Herself, a boy, and a half-wit Indian were no match for two well-armed desperadoes. This was no time for heroics. On the other hand if they knew what the boy had seen, they also knew that their cover as a couple of trail-weary cowpokes had flown out of the barn door with him. What's more, if one of them was wounded they wouldn't be fixing to ride on out as if nothing had happened: they'd be digging themselves in for an overnight stay at least. Then a thought occurred to her.

'Cal, you listen to me. Did they ask you anything about your pa?'

The boy sniffed and nodded.

'Asked me if I had a pa, and I told them I did.'

'Did they ask you where he was?'

'I told them he was away till tomorrow.'

Wilma Riley bit her lip in vexation. She had been contemplating using the threat of Jess's imminent return as a bargaining counter if there were any negotiating to do. But now the men knew they were safe from any interference.

'Tarnation!'

'Ma, I'm sorry,' said Cal looking at her anxiously.

'Never mind, Son. Wasn't your fault. I shouldn't have set you spying on them.'

She crossed quickly to the window and peered through the evening shadows at the barn door. There was no sign of movement.

'What are we going do, Ma?'

Wilma Riley paused again to consider. The obvious thing was to marshal their resources, but she didn't have much to marshal. Jess had taken the shotgun into town – not for protection, but because he liked to take a pot-shot at the occasional rabbit if he spotted one from the buckboard – so the only firearm she had was the six-shooter in the gunbelt hanging behind the door. Then there was Patch. Not exactly a ball of fire, but at least he had a knife and knew how to use it. Meantime how secure were they in this house? Only one door and one window in this main room. Beside the stove, a door led through to the only bedroom which had a window looking across the yard to the privy. Easy enough for a couple of well-armed people to defend, but with only one six-shooter she didn't rate her chances. Looked like Patch was her best chance, but where was he? She turned to the boy.

'Listen good, Cal. We've got to get word to Patch about what's happening. Do you know where he is?'

The boy shrugged. 'Last time I saw him he was seeing to the horses in the corral, but he wasn't there when I ran across from the barn, otherwise I would have called to him.'

Wilma clicked her tongue in irritation. 'Never knew such a one for disappearing when he's most needed. But maybe he's in the tackle-shed. Now listen, boy, he's our one chance. You skeeter out the side window and try and find him. They can't see you from the barn. Tell him to take any of the horses and make over to Jack Ellwood's spread for some help. No need for him to saddle up – I've seen him make it bareback when he wants to.'

Cal's mouth straightened with determination. 'OK, Ma. You just watch me.'

'Can't spare myself for that. I've got to watch that barn. And you listen good: stay out of sight and out of trouble whatever happens. If they catch you they'll have me hog-tied over a barrel and nothing to bargain with. You understand?'

'Sure, Ma. They won't get me.'

They went through into the bedroom. Wilma peered cautiously out of the window, released the catch and raised the sash enough for Cal to squirm his way through. She watched him scuttle away noiselessly across the yard and skirt round behind the outhouse. Then she fastened the window, closing and barring the wooden shutters behind it. She retraced her steps to the kitchen. Next priority was to check that six-shooter. Lord only knew how long it was since it had been last used. Jess Riley was no shooting man. She was just lifting down the gunbelt when there was a heavy pounding from the other side of the door.

'You in there, ma'am?'

Wilma recognized Abe's voice.

'I sure am,' she answered, trying to keep her voice steady and confident. 'And I've got a gun behind this door.'

'I only want to talk, ma'am. Ain't no call to go threatening like that.'

'Ain't no call to go hitting my boy like that, either.'

'That's my brother that done that, ma'am. He didn't mean nothing. The kid just got a bit sassy.'

There was a silence as Wilma waited to see what Abe was going to suggest next, while Abe put his head against the log panels of the door to try to hear if anything was going on inside.

'You still there, ma'am?' he called. 'We thought best thing was to come across and talk straight with you.'

'Best thing you can do, mister, is take your brother, get on your horses and ride on out of here. My boy told me all I need to know.'

'Ain't that simple, ma'am. The horses is tired and my brother isn't in a fit state to ride anyway. Guess you know that.'

'Guess I do. Can't sit a horse comfortable with a hole in his leg.'

'So it looks like you got us as guests whether you like it or not. Sure would be grateful if you'd open up this door real friendly-like, ma'am. Ain't no reason for us to be spitting lead at each other.'

Wilma edged herself towards the window and tried to

peer through a crack in the shutter. What she desperately wanted to hear was the sound of horse's hooves as Patch made a getaway. Surely Cal would have found him by now. But she couldn't make out any movement down by the corral. Meantime she needed to keep Abe's attention focused on the door. There was another heavy rap on the woodwork as Abe grew impatient.

'What do you say, ma'am? You planning to keep this door between us all night?'

'You got it in one, mister. Plus this, of course.'

Wilma held the revolver close to the door and gave the cylinder a few spins so that Abe could hear it clicking. There was a pause as Abe digested the unwelcome but useful information that she had at least one firearm in the house. Then she heard his boots clumping on the wooden boards of the stoop as he turned round and made his way back to the barn. Wilma heaved a sigh of relief. At least now, she'd have time to load this six-shooter – if she could remember how to do it. But where was that Indian, and why didn't he make his move?

Cal knew every inch of the Riley spread and he didn't figure it difficult to work his way round to the tackle-shed without being seen from the barn. Making a wide flanking circuit and using the various fences as cover it only took him a few minutes to reach the rear of the shed. Peering round the side wall he had a view of the front of the farmhouse with one of the strangers – it looked like Abe – standing at the door. There was no time to be lost. Besides the tackle and harnesses there was an alcove at the back of the shed where Patch bunked down at nights on a straw palliasse. He tapped lightly on the woodwork with a pebble to get the Indian's attention.

'Patch, Patch . . . it's me. You there, Patch?'

Cal held his breath, but there was no reply. He tried

again, without success. If Patch was doing what he seemed to do best – sleeping the sleep of the just – there was nothing for it but to go round the front and in through the door. Cautiously Cal poked his head round the side of the shed to check what was happening at the house. Abe had apparently given up and was walking back to the barn. This was the moment. Cal slipped round to the front of the shed, keeping as low as possible, and almost crawled through the doorway. The red beams of the sunset were glowing through the grime of the far window faintly illuminating the interior. In the gloom he could just make out the figure of Patch sprawled out on the floor. Cal grasped one of his feet and gave it a cautious twitch to wake him up without startling him.

'Patch, it's Cal. Wake up, will you?'

When the Indian still failed to respond, Cal crawled a little closer and saw the reason why. Patch's mouth was half open and slightly twisted, and there, in the dying rays of the sun, Cal could see the knife that had been thrust hilt-deep into his chest.

Stifling a yell of fear, the boy sat back on his heels and considered what to do next. . . .

'Seems to me there's no doubt about it,' said Seth when his brother reported back on what he'd heard through the farmhouse door. 'Since when did we get bested by a woman? We've got the Springfield, don't we? She's got the boy in there – no way she can risk a shoot-out.'

Abe scratched the stubble on his chin ruminatively. 'Well, maybe we ought to take a proper look round. Don't know how many points she's got to cover in that house till we see round the back.'

'How you going do that without her drawing a bead on you? She can cover us from that window.'

'You ain't thinking too good, Brother. Maybe that

liquor's soaked in up to your brain. How d'you reckon that boy got in here? He sure didn't come through the door.'

Abe glanced up at the loft. There had to be another way out. He climbed up the ladder, tested his weight carefully on the boards at the top, and then worked his way around until he came to the opening where Cal had squeezed in. He eased himself through headfirst to check that there was a way down. Then he swung himself around and clambered to the ground. As he'd anticipated, the side of the barn was out of view of the front of the house. He made his way across and scouted behind the house. No door, no window. He continued round the far side until he came to the bedroom window: closed, of course, and shuttered inside. He shook his head in irritation. Whoever built this place must have had Apache raids in mind. A couple of people could easily defend it against a war party, unless they were torched out.

Abe was standing pondering what to do next when a movement in the fading light down by the corral caught his eye. It was the boy about to hoist himself over the rail. And they'd thought he was in the house with his ma! Abe acted quickly. He drew his Colt and fired a single shot accurately into one of the corral standposts.

'Hold it right there, boy,' he yelled, as chips of the spruce-pole splintered by Cal's outstretched hand. 'You make one move and I'm gonna plug you real good.'

Cal froze in mid reach, startled by the closeness of the shot. Next thing he knew, Abe had come running up, seized him by the collar and almost lifted him around so that he was facing the house.

'Hey, Brother!' he yelled towards the barn. 'Come see what I caught.'

Parading the boy in front of him Abe approached the house as his brother limped out of the barn.

'You there, ma'am?' he enquired politely – knowing full

well that the woman could hardly have failed to hear the pistol shot. Keeping the boy in front of him with one hand, his Colt in the other, he stepped up on to the porch with Seth right beside him.

'Guess I'll have to ask you just one more time to open up real gently, ma'am. No need to tell you what's going to happen to your boy if you don't.'

There was a silence as Wilma Riley reluctantly faced the reality of the situation. Seth was getting impatient. He seized Cal from his brother and twisted his arm hard up behind his back. The boy's shriek of pain was enough to make up his mother's mind. There was a rattle as she unbarred the door which she then half opened cautiously.

'You lay off that boy, you hear,' said Wilma, appearing in the doorway with the six-shooter in her hand. 'He ain't done you no harm.'

'Thet's a matter of opinion, ma'am,' said Abe. 'I don't take kindly to having hot coffee flung in my face. Seems to me it's time somebody taught him some manners. My brother's real good at that.'

'Ma, Ma, they killed Patch! He's down there in the shed. I seen him.' Cal's voice was shrill with panic.

Wilma's lip curled as she contemplated the two men.

'You didn't have to do that. The Indian was harmless enough.'

'That's a matter of opinion, too, ma'am,' said Abe equably. 'Now are you going to let us in, or do I have to turn my brother loose on the boy?'

'Guess I've no choice.'

'Good thinking. Now just slide that gun across to me real steady and we'll be ready to accept your kind offer of hospitality.'

Wilma stooped down and kicked the gun across the boards where it fetched up at Abe's feet. He picked it up and motioned her inside. Seth slammed the door shut behind them and released his grip on Cal, sending him sprawling headfirst on the floor.

'You sure could have saved us all this trouble, ma'am.'

'Just say what you want, mister, and leave us in peace. There ain't nothing here for you. My husband took all the spare cash into town with him.'

'Cash isn't exactly our problem, ma'am. But a good night's rest sure is.'

Abe glanced over her shoulder through the open door of the bedroom, 'Seems to me you got exactly what we want. Nice feather bed and the right sort of company to keep it warm.'

'You low-down skunk. Don't you talk like that in front of the boy.' Abe chuckled. Then he turned to his brother and pointed at a washing rope coiled up alongside the stove. 'Tie the kid up, Seth. No need for him to watch while his ma and I transact business.' Seth took the rope, thrust the wriggling boy on to a heavy oak chair that was standing in one corner, and tied him securely to it round arms and torso.

'Now, ma'am,' said Abe, hanging up his hat and loosening his belt, 'we'll just show you how well brought up me and my brother are. We take everything in turns – real polite-like.'

He pushed her roughly inside the bedroom and threw her on to the bed. She struggled like a wildcat, but he was too strong for her. Cal writhed helplessly against his bonds as his mother's screams sounded through the house. . . .

There was no clock in the kitchen and the single oil lamp was burning low, but Cal reckoned it must be past midnight. His mother had stopped screaming long since, but he had wanted to make sure that both men were sound asleep before he made his move. The rope that was securing him to the chair was bound tightly round his arms, but his hands had been left free and a couple of hours of cautious wriggling had resulted in enough leeway to manoeuvre one hand inside his dungarees. Carefully he extracted the knife which he had removed from the dead Apache's body. Then he used it to cut himself loose from the chair. He glanced around. One of the men was still in the bedroom, the other was stretched out on Cal's own bed in the alcove beside the hearth. Cal stood up and tiptoed across the room. They hadn't even bothered to bar the door. He let himself out and made his way cat-like in the moonlight across to the barn. His boots were where he had left them that afternoon. He put them on, took a few minutes to take care of something else that he had planned while tied up inside, and then hightailed it out across country.

FOUR

Hank Sefton woke later than he'd intended. Sheriff Westlake had made the most of his opportunity to while away an otherwise solitary evening with his reluctant detainee, and it had been past midnight when he'd finally opened the cell door to let him out.

So it was well after eight when he walked across to Nelson's Livery Stables to see about fixing himself up with a mount for the next few days. At first sight the prospects didn't look too good. Just a couple of rangy geldings and a pinto with a distinctly hostile eye.

'You looking for something, mister?'

Old man Nelson had appeared from out back carrying a couple of buckets of feed.

'I was kind of hoping to find a horse to hire for a few days. Need to ride out of town aways.'

Nelson pursed his lips as he sized him up with a professional eye.

'Can't say as I'd recommend either of them geldings. You might find them sagging in the middle after a coupla miles. Now the paint might suit you – if you can stick on him, that is.'

'Any reason why I shouldn't?'

'Nope. 'Cept that it's kind of difficult when he's up on his hind legs most of the time.' Nelson chuckled. 'Tell you

39

what I'll do, mister. I'll fetch you a nice Mexican saddle with a big strong horn to hold on to. That way you can slide off real gentle whenever you feels like it.'

Sefton didn't care much for the old man's jokes but there didn't seem to be any choice. They got a rope round the pinto's neck and harnessed him up without either of them getting kicked. He looked meaner by the minute, especially when they tightened the girth strap.

'All right, mister – he's all yours. Care to mount up?'

'Not yet. What's his name?'

'Rayo.'

'That because he moves like a flash?'

'Maybe. Or because he bucks like flash.'

Sefton walked round to the horse's head and spent a few minutes stroking its nose and talking softly to it. Then he nodded to the old man who took a firm hold of the face strap while Sefton swung himself carefully into the saddle. The horse bucked violently, and even though Sefton had been expecting it he found himself unseated. Only a desperate clutch at the saddle horn saved him from going down under the horse's hooves.

'Told you, mister. You want to change your mind?'

Sefton answered the challenge with a contemptuous look and remounted. This time he hung on as the horse bucked and reared. Two minutes later he was still in the saddle and old man Nelson's expression had become a sight more respectful.

'Seems like you knows something about horses, mister.'

'Guess so. I've been trail riding since I was fifteen. I'll take him for a couple of days anyway to see how he shapes out. How much?'

'Twenny-five for the horse and thirty for the saddle.'

'Fifty-five bucks for a bronco that nobody else could ride? I could buy him outright for a hundred.'

Nelson spat dispassionately on the ground.

'No you couldn't. I'd be asking more than that. He's a good horse for the right rider.'

'All right,' said Sefton. He was over a barrel and the old man knew it. 'But I want a receipt.'

Half an hour later with his saddle roll behind him he was out on the trail with Rayo set in a steady trot. It was a few years since he'd last been this way, but he remembered the main features. He kept the three rocks from which the town drew its name on his left and headed through the low hills towards Salto Creek.

After an hour on the trail it felt as though he and Rayo were old friends. Having apparently accepted that Sefton was going to be a difficult customer to dislodge, the horse was proving a willing partner. He needed no urging, and maintained a steady and sure footed pace with his ears well pricked forwards. Sefton was just congratulating himself on his choice of mount when, for once, Rayo seemed momentarily to check his pace. As the horse's ears flicked backwards and forwards a couple of times Sefton thought he could hear, somewhere in the far distance, an exchange of gunshots. He pulled Rayo up and listened for a moment, but there was nothing to break the silence but the occasional birdcall. Assuming that he must have heard some local farmer potting jack-rabbits, Sefton rode on. Almost imperceptibly the scrub and thorn bushes gave way to a greener landscape of prairie grass and cottonwoods as the trail descended steadily towards the creek. Sefton figured it might be a good place to stop and rest the horse a while. Then he saw that somebody else seemed to have had the same idea. A buckboard was skewed off the road beneath some trees and the horse was cropping the vegetation.

Sefton slowed the pinto down and circled the buckboard. At first he thought its owner must have made his way down to the creek, but as he completed the circuit he

realized that the truth was more sinister. The body of a
man lay sprawled face down in the dirt. Sefton glanced
around and then dismounted, tying Rayo to the wagon.
He walked up to the body and crouched over it. The man's
hat had become dislodged and was lying a few feet away.
Sefton tentatively stretched out his fingers to where a
tangled of matted bloodstained hair revealed that the
corpse had been shot through the head.

'Well, I'll be hog-tied,' he murmured to himself.

He took a moment to wipe his face with his kerchief.
Then he carefully grasped the dead man's shoulder and
rolled him over slightly so as to get a sight of his face. As
the man's profile lifted into view Sefton recoiled, almost
as though reacting to a rattlesnake's strike, and stumbled
to his feet. Despite the heat of the morning he suddenly
started to shiver. As he stood there trying to make sense
of what he was seeing he became aware of the sound
of galloping hooves approaching up the trail from
Salto. . . .

Saturday morning breakfast at the Double L was usually a
tense affair. Friday nights might offer the opportunity of a
little amusement in town, but Saturday was a working day
like any other, and Jack Ellwood made no concessions to
his sons: there was no question of a lie-in while others
worked.

Pat Ellwood groaned, swung himself into a seated position on his bed and groped for his boots. The breakfast
horn had sounded and it didn't pay to be more than a
couple of minutes late making an appearance at table. He
pulled on his boots, ran his hand through his hair and
walked through to the kitchen. He was still wearing the
clothes he'd had on last night, but he could change later
after he'd faced his father. His sister Kathy was already
spooning the griddle cakes out of the pan and had bacon

sizzling alongside. It was an unbeatable combination – any morning but Saturdays.

'Just coffee for me, Sis.'

Jack Ellwood glanced at the clock as he followed his son into the kitchen.

'Where's your brother?'

Pat shrugged but made no reply. Mike could offer his own explanations for being late.

Ellwood sat down at the table and started his breakfast without making any further comment. He was just reaching for the coffee when there was a knock on the kitchen door and Chuck Morrison appeared with his hand in a bandage.

'What in tarnation happened to you?' Ellwood's tone conveyed no hint of sympathy.

'Some saddle-bum shot his gun out of his hand last night, Pa,' said Pat, as the events of the previous evening came back sharply into focus.

'You hold your goddammed tongue, boy. I wasn't asking you. My foreman's capable of speaking for himself. That's what I pay him for.'

'It's true, Mr Ellwood. Sonofabitch accused me of cheating him at cards and then tried shooting me up.'

'Looks like he made a neat job of it. Guess you won't be trying any of your fancy dealing tricks with that hand for a while.'

'No, Mr Ellwood. And that's what I came to see you about. It's going to be kind of hard roping steers with my hand like this for a few days.'

Ellwood took a long swig of coffee and then sat back in his chair and stared hard at his foreman.

'That's your problem, Chuck. You know my rules. No work, no pay. Best get yourself back to the bunkhouse and nurse that hand if it's bothering you. You can send Gus Donovan over here. Tell him he's foreman till further notice. Now, get.'

'I didn't mean it like that, Mr Ellwood. It's only going to be a day or so, I swear. There's other jobs I can be doing.'

'Forget it, Chuck. Foreman with a busted hand ain't no use to me. Think yourself lucky I'm still willing to keep you on as a cowhand. If it doesn't suit, you know what you can do.'

Ellwood resumed his breakfast while Morrison slunk out of the kitchen with a sideways glance at Pat which suggested a mute appeal for support. But Pat kept his eyes on his coffee cup, making no intervention on Morrison's behalf. Mike's chair was still empty and there was a further storm to come. Ellwood was just pushing his chair back from the table when his younger son appeared.

'Sorry, pa. Overslept.'

'Late night, huh?' asked Ellwood encouragingly.

'Kind of.'

'Well, don't you worry, boy. Take all the time to sleep that you want. Best get yourself back to bed.'

'It's all right, Pa, I'll work extra tonight, I promise.'

Mike made to sit himself at the table, but his father kicked the chair away from him.

'Work starts at six o'clock on this ranch, mister, and you're no exception. Now take your hide back to your room. I'm docking you a day's pay.'

'Aw, please, Pa. I said I'm sorry.'

'Just get out of here. Next time this happens you'll be spreading your bedroll in the bunkhouse.'

As Mike retreated to his room, Ellwood strode out on to the porch. He glanced impatiently towards the bunk-house, looking for Gus Donovan, but another figure came running towards him.

'Now what in. . . ?'

Hearing the astonishment in Ellwood's voice Kathy and Pat came out to stand behind him. Next minute Cal Riley came running up and almost fell at their feet.

'Please, Mr Ellwood,' he gasped. 'I need help real bad. They got Mom and Patch and they nearly got me. . . .'

'Hold it, son,' grunted Ellwood, grabbing him by the shoulders and guiding him indoors. 'Let's hear you out properly. Calm down.'

Kathy Ellwood shook her head in disbelief. 'Just look at the state of him.'

The boy was scarcely recognizable as the Cal Riley they knew as their closest neighbour's son. His clothes were torn, his boots were filthy and his face was swollen and streaked with grime. They brought him into the kitchen, sat him down and listened as he panted out his story. When he had finished, the Ellwoods exchanged glances over the boy's head.

'Looks like we've got real trouble around here,' murmured Ellwood. 'Kathy, you look after the boy. Give him breakfast, clean him up and put him to bed. Pat, you and I'd best get down to the Riley place. You can get your brother out of his room and tell him to ride in to Three Rocks for Sheriff Westlake. Look sharp, you hear?'

'Yes, Pa. Thanks.'

Pat hurried off to let his brother know he was sprung from confinement while Ellwood gave a rather surprised and bewildered Gus Donovan his orders for the day. Less than five minutes later Jack and Pat Ellwood were heading across country towards the Riley spread. They made their journey in silence apart from the panting of their horses as they kept them up to a sharp pace. They took the fastest and most direct route, diverting from the main track where there was any chance of saving distance and time. Jack Ellwood couldn't help marvelling at what Cal Riley had apparently accomplished last night. If the boy was telling the truth and had actually covered the distance on foot through the hours of darkness, there must have been an unseen hand looking after him. It was an uncomfortable ride even in broad daylight. For a boy of scarce thirteen years on foot it must have been a real test of strength and willpower.

'There it is, Pa!'

Pat reined in his horse as they came over the bluffs and the farmstead was revealed below them.

'Seems peaceful enough,' said Pat.

Apart from the horses in the corral, which looked like Jess Riley's, there was no movement down below and no sound of life.

'Best take it easy from now on in,' ordered Jack. 'If there's anyone down there they'll see us as soon as we get to the bottom.'

They picked their way quietly and carefully towards the creek, keeping a careful watch for any movement from the farmhouse or the outbuildings. At the gate they paused again, but the silence was total.

'OK, Son. Guess we go on in.'

They rode through the gate and approached the house. Jack Ellwood dismounted and handed Pat the reins of his horse.

'I'll go in by myself, just in case.'

He drew his revolver and made his way quietly up to the door. Standing slightly to one side he kicked the unlatched door wide open and peered inside.

The kitchen showed signs of disturbance. A chair had been overturned and there was smashed crockery on the stone floor. There was no fire in the stove. Ellwood stepped across to the door leading to the bedroom and pushed it slightly open. The shutters to the bedroom window were still closed and he found it difficult to see anything. He pushed the door wide open allowing light to flood in from the kitchen. As the light illuminated the bed, Jack paused long enough to satisfy himself of the truth, and then retraced his steps quickly outside.

'What's been goin' on, Pa?'

Pat's voice was nervous. The general stillness of the place was disquieting.

Ellwood shook his head.

'It's Wilma. They throttled her with a length of rope. God knows what they did to her first. Judging by the state of the room she must have put up a heck of a struggle. It's a wonder that kid didn't go off his head.'

Ellwood sighed. It was a job for the sheriff – and good luck to him with the trail going colder by the minute.

'I guess we'd better check the outbuildings while we're here.'

It was Pat who found the Apache. Flat on his back with a knife wound in his chest just as the boy had said. The flies were buzzing round him already. When they'd seen all there was to be seen Ellwood checked his watch.

'Getting on for mid morning. According to the kid Jess should be on his way back from Three Rocks with the buckboard. I sure wouldn't like him to come across all this without warning. Guess we'd better ride toward Salto Creek till we meet up with him.'

'But Pa, what are we gonna say to him when we meet up? I ain't never had to break this sort of news to anyone in my life.'

'Think it's a regular event for me, boy? I suppose the words'll come out right enough when the moment arrives. Let's get going.'

Gus Donovan took a few minutes to digest the implications of Chuck Morrison's sudden demotion. Then he made his way to the Double L bunkhouse to detail off the work force for the day. Word of the excitement over at the Riley place had already reached the hands, but Mr Ellwood would expect a full day's work at the ranch with no excuses. The newly acquired responsibility would not lie heavily on his shoulders. Donovan had played second fiddle to Chuck Morrison for longer than he cared to remember and there wasn't much he didn't know about ranching, or about Jack Ellwood's view of Morrison's relationship with his sons. Ellwood tolerated the boys moseying into town on Friday nights to blow their week's pay on cards, booze and women, but all the hands knew that he had nothing but contempt for their behaviour. Except Chuck Morrison. Supposedly his role in these outings was to keep the two boys in some sort of control and out of trouble, but he was too scared of them to exercise any authority – and his weakness did nothing for him in Ellwood's eyes.

Donovan ignored Morrison until he'd given instructions to the other cattle-prodders, then he turned to where the ex-foreman was sitting disconsolately on his bunk nursing his injured hand.

'Guess we'd better keep you busy one way or the other today, Chuck. You ain't going to be much use for cattle work but I guess you can always use a broom left-handed. You can give this bunkhouse a right good scouring for a start. Smells as high as a hog house. Then you can start clearing the trash out of the corral. Time it was cleaned up properly.'

Morrison scowled up at him in disbelief.

'Just what do you think you're doing, Gus? That's woman's work in here, and Injun's work outside you just given me, you sonofabitch. Who do you think you are?'

'Jack Ellwood's foreman until further notice,' said Donovan calmly. 'Now get off that bunk and get to work.'

Morrison glanced around at the handful of cowboys who had lingered to smirk at this deliberate humiliation and allowed his temper to explode.

'Why, you low-heeled lump of buzzard-bait, I'll learn ya to give me orders like that!'

He launched himself from his bunk and before the startled Donovan could do anything to defend himself he
whipped his boot hard into Donovan's stomach. As
Donovan folded with a grunt Morrison brought his knee
up under Donovan's chin accurately enough to make
Donovan's jaw rattle. The acting-foreman went down with
a crash on the dusty pine-boards and Morrison was over
him in a moment drawing his boot back to land another
stunner on Donovan's head.

Up to now Morrison had had the advantage of surprise,
but Donovan was a quick thinker who was only dealing
with a one-handed opponent. He rolled adroitly to one
side as Morrison's boot came down, grasped his foot and
twisted it with almost enough force to break his ankle.
Morrison yelled, lost his balance, and crashed to the floor.
In normal circumstances Donovan wouldn't even have
considered lowering himself to fight with a man who had
an injured hand. But there was a coveted foreman's job at
stake and, besides, it was Morrison who had struck the first
blow. If he chose to pick a fight with only one good hand
he had to take the consequences. Donovan scrambled up,
hauled the grimacing Morrison to his feet and threw him
hard enough against one of the walls of the bunkhouse to
knock the breath out of his lungs. Then, as Morrison
sagged helplessly up against the clapboard, Donovan
thumped his fists methodically, left and right, into every
part of his body, giving him, in full view of the assembled
company, a comprehensive hammering, while contriving
not to inflict any serious structural damage. Nobody spoke
or came to Morrison's assistance in the two or three
minutes it took Donovan to complete the demonstration
of his newly acquired authority.

When he had finished and had allowed Morrison to
drop, retching and groaning, on the floor Donovan stood
back and looked down at him contemptuously. 'You've got

a choice now, Chuck. You pick up the mop and clean up
your own puke or you hightail it out of here.'

As he staggered to his feet, Morrison's face revealed
that he understood the reality of the situation. All the
vestiges of his authority had been stripped away with the
thumping he'd just been provoked into taking. There
wasn't a man on the ranch who would ever take an order
from him again.

'Damn your hide, Donovan. You've got what you
wanted and I'm outa here for good. But don't make the
mistake of thinking you've seen the last of me: I ain't never
going to forget what you've just done. Better watch your
back for the rest of your hog-rotten life, mister – as long as
it lasts!'

As if to prove that Morrison's threat was empty
Donovan turned away and called the other cowhands to
duty.

'Come on, boys, some of us have got real work to do.
Let's get to it!'

Left alone in the silence of the bunkhouse Chuck
Morrison gathered his few possessions together and made
his way out to the corral to saddle up his horse. The bay
gelding, the contents of his saddle roll, his stock whip and
a few dollars in his pocket were all he had to show for close
on twelve years' grinding work on the Double L. Now he
was due nothing, so there were no goodbyes. He paused
under the arched spruce-poles that marked the entrance
to the ranch and considered where he was going to head.
Three Rocks was nearest, of course, but word would soon
be around that he'd been ousted. He didn't fancy the pity-
ing looks he'd be getting in the saloon – and anyway he
owed too much on the tab to risk a rebuff. So it would
have to be Sedona Springs. He turned the gelding's head
north-west and dug in his spurs.

FIVE

Sefton stepped out from the shadow of the trees to wave down the approaching horsemen. The two men trotted up and halted by the dead body.

'What in tarnation's been going on here?' asked the younger of the two.

Jack Ellwood dismounted and studied the corpse. 'It's Riley, Pat. Shot through the head.'

Pat Ellwood drew his Colt and levelled it at Sefton.

'Best raise your hands, mister. Looks like you got some explaining to do.'

'Now wait a minute,' protested Sefton. 'I just got here. I'm not even armed. My gunbeit's in my saddle roll.'

As Sefton spoke, Pat Ellwood suddenly recognized him from last night's card game. He fanned back the hammer on his pistol menacingly.

'Pa, this is the saddle-bum who shot Chuck up last night.'

'That so?'

'Sure is. Looks like he's a real prairie skunk. I can smell 'em a mile off.'

Jack Ellwood studied Sefton for a moment and then turned to his son.

'Put your gun away, coyote-brain. Jess here was killed with a rifle shot through the head. I don't see any rifle around here, do you?'

As Pat reluctantly holstered his six-shooter, Ellwood eyed Sefton a little more closely. 'Say, son, you look kind of familiar. Have we ever met before?'

'Maybe,' said Sefton. 'I'm Wilma Riley's brother, Hank Sefton.'

Ellwood gave a low whistle and slapped his thigh.

'I knew I'd seen you. Wilma's kid brother. Why I haven't clapped eyes on you since you were knee high to a racoon. Remember me? Jack Ellwood?'

'Can't say as I do. But I've been riding the range since I was fifteen. Few weeks ago I got a letter from my sister saying it was high time I came for a visit so I hung up my spurs and took the stage up from Yuma.'

Pat Ellwood stared from one to the other as he absorbed this unexpected information.

'But, but that makes you. . . .'

He gestured down at the corpse that lay between them. Sefton stared back at him with a level gaze.

'That's right. That makes me Jess Riley's brother-in-law.'

After a few seconds' silence, Sefton turned his attention back to the figure of the dead man. Maybe they ought to cover him. It didn't look decent sprawled out in the heat and dust. Then a thought occurred to him. He buried his face in his hands.

'What am I going to say to Wilma?'

Jack Ellwood put a hand on his shoulder.

'Son, why don't we sit down on the buckboard. I've got something to tell you. And I'm afraid it isn't pleasant. . . .'

They had left the trail well before it approached Three Rocks. Abe had figured it out, of course. By cutting off north-west they could head for Sedona Springs and then the Santa Fe railhead some twenty miles beyond it. From there he reckoned it would be easy enough to disappear well out of the reach of any posse.

A half day of rough riding over bare sun-baked scarps broken by occasional rocky outcrops brought them to the crest of a summit where they found themselves looking down on a wooded gulch with a trickle of fresh water glinting through the stunted undergrowth. They picked their way down the escarpment and tethered their sweating horses in a scrap of shade beneath an overhang of sandstone after letting them quench their thirst in the arroyo. Seth limped over to a shallow pool and splashed water over his head and neck.

'How much time you reckon we got?'

'Enough. That trail ain't exactly main street. Could be best part of a day before anyone finds that buckboard.'

'Still don't see why you had to kill him. He wasn't no threat.'

Abe looked at his brother contemptuously.

'That how you see it? We kazoo his wife every which way, and you think he ain't about to move heaven and earth to bring us down? We were lucky to run into him before we turned off the trail. Anyway, it doesn't much matter: it's just the first killing that counts. They can only hang you once, Brother.'

They sprawled out on the shingle, scoffing some of the rye bread and preserves they'd lifted from the homestead before taking off that morning. Abe felt in his shirt pocket and pulled out a cheroot. Some dollar bills which he'd lifted from Riley's body on the trail earlier fluttered to the ground.

'Guess it was our lucky day,' he grinned, gathering them into his fist. 'Might as well stash them with the others.'

He stood up, walked over to his horse, and unstrapped one of the saddle pouches. Suddenly a scream of rage followed by a volley of oaths echoed around the gulch as Abe spun round, his Colt already in his hand.

'Why you dirty, cheap, little sidewinder. What kind of crooked deal do you think you're pulling, mister?'

'What in tarnation's going on for Pete's sake?' yelled Seth, stumbling to his feet.

'This!' snarled Abe, reaching in to the saddle pouch with his free hand and pulling out a handful of straw. He kept his eyes and his pistol trained on his brother. 'What have you done with it, Seth?'

His brother looked frightened and bewildered.

'Abe, I swear I ain't done nothing. Far as I knew, the money was stashed in the bags when we took off this morning. It was all there last night.'

'Well it ain't there now, you little, two-bit trail-louse.'

Seth sank to his knees as Abe fanned back the hammer on his Colt. The range was point blank and he knew from bitter experience that his brother was remorseless.

'I swear I ain't touched it, Abe. You know I wouldn't two-time you. It must have been the kid done the switch before he lit off.'

There was a terrible pause as Abe digested this analysis while keeping the pistol levelled at Seth's head. Then he stepped forward to where his brother was quivering on his knees in the dirt.

'And whose fault was that? You were the one who couldn't even tie a kid up secure.'

'And you were the one who wouldn't let me finish him off like I wanted.'

As he saw his brother's jaw tighten at this comeback Seth made another plea. 'Please, Abe, don't—'

His words were cut off abruptly as Abe reversed his hold on the Colt with a flick of his hand so as to grasp it by the muzzle. Then he brought the butt down sideways with a vicious swipe across Seth's face.

Seth moaned as the force of the blow knocked him over.

'What did you do that for?' he gasped as he clutched at the injured side of his face. 'I told you it wasn't me.'

'Because you're a useless lump of horse flesh with a cactus for a brain. The boy must have seen you take the money out when he was keyholing in the barn. You shouldn't have touched it. And you should have checked the pouches this morning. Do I have to think of everything?'

'I'm sorry, Abe,' whimpered Seth. 'Can I get up now?'

'I ought to make you crawl for the rest of the day, mister. All right, on your feet.'

Seth stood up and gingerly removed his hand from his face. It was covered in blood from a cut across his temple.

'Now see what you've done. You've gone and scarred me up, as if I wasn't in enough trouble with my leg.'

'Quit bellyaching: it's only a scratch.'

Seth pulled his bandanna from around his neck and held it to his head to staunch the bleeding.

'What we going to do now?'

Abe stared at his brother in disgust. He made no reply, but perched himself on a convenient rock and began to throw stones aimlessly into the arroyo. Twenty-four hours ago they'd had enough money under their saddles to last them a year with careful living. Now, all they had to their credit was a string of corpses and a boy who was still alive to identify them as his mother's killers. It seemed as though their plans needed an overhaul already.

By the time Jack Ellwood had finished telling Sefton the story of last night's happenings at the Riley homestead, a cloud of dust on the trail from Three Rocks heralded the arrival of Sheriff Westlake, Mike Ellwood and a couple of stray cowpokes deputized at short notice.

Westlake reined in his sorrel and then edged it cautiously, almost disbelievingly, over to the buckboard where they'd laid out Jess Riley's body.

'Holy cow. Someone's been real busy around here.'

'Happened about an hour ago as far as we can make out,' said Ellwood. He indicated Sefton, who was standing nearby. 'This feller found him on the road with a rifle shot clean through his head. Sheriff, this is—'

'I know who he is,' said Westlake, nodding at Sefton. 'He was my guest for supper last night.'

He turned towards Sefton. 'I'm real sorry about this, mister. Kind of a terrible homecoming for you. Things like this don't normally happen around these parts.'

Hank Sefton's expression reflected his mood: cold anger mixed with self-reproach. 'If only I'd been a day earlier, things might have been different.'

'No good nursing regrets, Sefton,' said Westlake. 'No way you could ever have guessed what was going to happen.'

Pat Ellwood glanced impatiently at his brother.

'How long we gonna stand around here gassing, Sheriff? Trail's going cold by the minute.'

'Don't steam your britches off, Pat. A bit of cool thinking never did any harm.'

'Any idea who these desperadoes are, Sheriff?' asked Ellwood. 'All Cal's boy could tell us was that he thought they were brothers and one of them's got a wounded leg.'

'Can't be absolutely certain, but I can make a fair guess. Abe and Seth Lancing. Turned over a bank in Halesville couple of days ago. Killed the cashier and made off with nearly three thousand bucks. Bank teller thinks he managed to wing one of them. I had a wire about it yesterday.'

'Question is,' mused Ellwood, 'which way they headed? We didn't see nobody on our way from the Riley place, and Hank didn't meet them riding in from Three Rocks.'

'They must have turned off the trail somewhere

between here and town,' said Westlake. 'We'd better head back and try and pick up their tracks. Ain't going to be easy.'

He turned to one of his deputies. 'You stay here, Newt. Take the buckboard, get some help at Salto and fetch Wilma's body back to town. Rest of us'll do some scouting. Keep behind me, gentlemen. Don't want you scuffling up the trail any more than it is already.'

Westlake led the way at a steady trot. Even if they found the point where the Lancings had turned off, it was going to be a slow job following them across country. Ten minutes back along the trail they found where the Lancings had struck off on their own route. From then on, as Westlake had feared, it was hard going. They hadn't gone a mile when he found himself forced to retrace their steps at Sefton's bidding.

'You've gone wrong, Sheriff,' he said pointing out the tell-tale signs of broken twigs and disturbed shale that betrayed the path that the Lancings had taken.

'Pretty darned good at this, aren't you, Sefton?' grinned Westlake after Sefton had made the third correction to his intended path.

'Try to be,' said Sefton laconically. 'Cattle driving teaches you a thing or two.'

Westlake nodded and reined back discreetly to let Sefton make the running. Even so, progress was slow. Sefton knew from experience that tracking was a job you couldn't hurry, but back behind him Pat and Mike Ellwood were getting restless at the constant stops as Sefton and the sheriff examined the ground. Every time they reached the crest of a summit all eyes scanned the horizon in the hope of spotting a tell-tale sign of movement somewhere below but there was never anything to be seen.

They were skirting the edge of a mesa when Mike Ellwood called over to him.

'Hey mister, you sure you're not leading us in circles? Seems kind of funny we ain't spotted them yet.'

'Pipe down, boy,' snarled his father. 'Tracking ain't kid's stuff. If you can't take it, turn your goddam horse around and make off for home.'

'Assuming you can find it on your own,' sniggered his brother.

'Sure I can find it. We left a clear enough trail behind us.'

Mike Ellwood turned in his saddle to point out their tracks just as his horse stumbled against a loose rock pitching him violently to the ground. With a yell of surprise and then a scream of real fear he rolled to the edge of the mesa and disappeared from view.

'Son-of-a-gun,' muttered Jack Ellwood springing off his horse.

'Mike, Mike, are you down there?' He advanced cautiously to the edge, testing his weight against the firmness of the rock.

'Pa, I'm here.'

Mike's voice came faintly back from somewhere below. They all dismounted and joined Ellwood senior to peer cautiously downwards. The youngster was sprawled out on a narrow ledge about ten feet below them, with no obvious means of getting back up, clutching desperately with one hand to a slender stunted tree root.

'Help me, Pa. Please. I don't think I can hold on to this for long.'

One of his legs was already dangling off into mid air and threatening to unbalance the rest of his body. Sefton sized up the situation and saw what was needed. He turned to Pat Ellwood.

'You got a lariat under your saddle. Let's have it quick.'

He took the rope, fastened one end to the pommel of Rayo's saddle and threw the noosed end down to Ellwood on the ledge. He motioned Pat Ellwood to hold the pinto steady.

'Can you get this under your arms, boy?'

'I'll try, mister.'

Mike wriggled his free arm and head through the loop but had to change his grip on the stump to get his other arm through. As he shifted his weight the edge of the outcrop crumbled beneath him. With a scream he tipped over in a shower of dust and the rope went slack.

'Moses,' muttered Jack Ellwood. 'He's gone.'

'Not yet,' said Sefton peering through the dust. He could just see Mike's hands clinging desperately to what was left of the ledge. But his head and body were out of sight. Sefton hurriedly pulled in the rope and slipped it over his own shoulders.

'Lower me down real careful,' he snapped to Pat Ellwood.

As Ellwood paid out the rope Sefton went backwards over the edge and walked himself slowly down the rock face to where Mike was holding on. Swivelling his head he could see the boy's face – white with fear and the near certainty of imminent death.

'Can you help me out of this, mister?' Ellwood pleaded. 'I'm sorry about what happened last night. Please do something. I can't hold on much longer.'

Sefton managed to get a toe hold on the remains of the ledge and crouched down facing outwards.

'Take the strain on that rope up there, you hear? I'm going to try pulling him up.'

He extended his left hand to Ellwood's right and established a hand-over-hand grip. Then he did the same with his other hand.

'Pull, up there, for Pete's sake!' he shouted.

As the combined strength of the four men and the horse up above pulled Sefton's shoulders upright he could hear Mike Ellwood's boots scrabbling desperately for a purchase against the cliff face. Slowly, held by Sefton's vice-like grip, he reappeared over the edge until they were both standing precariously on the ledge.

'All right,' called Ellwood, flat on his stomach peering over from above. 'Here comes another lariat.'

A second noose came snaking down and was slipped over Mike Ellwood's shoulders. With both of them secured it was only a matter of minutes to haul them both up. Mike Ellwood lay prostrate for a moment shaking with fear and exhaustion.

'Guess you owe this *caballero* a thank-ye,' remarked his father.

Mike struggled gasping to his feet. 'Thanks mister,' he mumbled, addressing Sefton's boots. 'Sure appreciate what you did.' Matt Westlake surveyed the skyline and pursed his lips.

'All very well, gentlemen, but the show's over for today, I think. We're too far behind to have any chance of over-hauling them Lancings. Guess we'll have to call it a day.'

'Oh, come on, Sheriff,' protested Sefton. 'They're my sister's killers. You going to let them get away?'

'Nope,' said Westlake. 'But there's more than one way of skinning a cat. Sun'll be going down in a couple of hours. You fancy spending the night out here?'

Sefton shook his head in exasperation. 'Wouldn't be the first time I've overnighted in the saddle.' He gestured back at his saddle roll. 'At least I'm equipped for it. Now look, Sheriff, this may be just another case to you but I just lost a sister and brother-in-law. I'm not giving up till I see the skunks that did it swinging at the end of a rope.'

'Like I told you last night, son, you sure do sound off some,' said Westlake. 'But the fact is we've lost too much time and they've gained too much ground. We aren't equipped to track them in the dark, so I'm not about to embark on any wild goose chase. You can please yourself, of course.'

'Sheriff's right, Hank,' said Ellwood. 'Best thing you can do is come back with us to the ranch. We can do some more thinking in the morning when we're fresh.'

Sefton stared at him with a pang of guilt. Ellwood's words had suddenly reminded him that he had a nephew waiting there – and that the boy was now an orphan.

SIX

'You look kind of lonely, mister.'

Belle Dunnett perched herself on a bar stool next to the stranger and hitched up her flounced red satin skirt high enough to reveal a well-turned ankle and a fair measure of black-stockinged leg as well.

Chuck Morrison glared at her balefully and swallowed his whiskey in one gulp. He knew enough about saloons to be aware that however lonely a man was, the company of a woman like Belle was going to have to be paid for. He'd loped into Sedona Springs late that afternoon with less than a hundred bucks in his pocket, a body that ached from the long day's one-handed ride and the beating he'd suffered at Donovan's hands that morning, and a mind that burned with resentment at the treatment he'd suffered at the Double L ranch. He banged his empty glass down loudly on the bar counter.

'Same again!'

'Care to buy a girl a drink, mister?' Belle persisted.

Morrison scowled. 'Later maybe.'

'Please yourself,' said Belle, huffily. She stood up, abruptly. 'My name's Belle. I'll be around.'

'Sure you will.'

Morrison managed a wry grin as Belle looked him over with a professional eye. He was fairly good-looking in a rather trail-worn way, but there were bruises on his face and a bandage on one hand. Her tone suddenly turned motherly instead of sisterly.

'You look done in, mister. Just off the trail?'

'Yup.'

Morrison continued to study his glass, obstinately disinclined to make things easy for her. But Belle persisted.

'Thought I hadn't seen you around here before. Looking for work?'

'Maybe.'

'What kind?'

'Ranch hand. Cattle herding. That sort of thing.'

Suddenly as the second whiskey began to take effect he could feel the alcohol coursing through his bloodstream. As his morale lifted, so did his willingness to converse.

'You know of anything going in that line around here?' he asked.

'Well,' Belle drawled, 'it's all good cattle-ranging country to the north of here so there's always hands needed. You look like you've got experience.'

'Guess I have at that,' said Morrison with a perceptible trace of bitterness in his voice.

'Best way of finding out what's needed is you go and chew the fat with the local cowboys.' She nodded over to the far corner where there were a couple of raucous card games in progress.

'You a card player, mister?'

'I've played some.'

'Why don't you go over and try your luck. You never know – you might get yourself a job and a few pots.'

She leant forward and squeezed his knee encouragingly. A pang of acute physical pleasure shot through Morrison, reminding him how long it was since he had enjoyed real female company. Then he brushed her hand away and swivelled round to survey the card games. After a few moments he turned back to Belle with a slight smile.

'Guess I might just take your advice, ma'am.'

He tipped his hat politely towards her. If he got lucky he might be glad of her services later.

'Please, call me Belle.'

'All right. Belle.'

Morrison grinned, stood up and rattled a couple of coins down on the counter. Then he walked over to the noisier of the two card games.

'You got room for one more?'

One of the hayseeds looked up and nodded. 'Sure, mister. More the merrier.'

He shifted his chair a little to make room for Morrison at the table.

'Name's Al, pardner – and this here's Carl, Ash and Zeke.'

He indicated the players on either side of him. There were two others at the table but no introductions were made. Morrison sat down and cautiously passed a few hands while he studied the hayseeds, who were clearly playing for fun, and the two men opposite who looked like serious opposition.

The ill-shaven card player across the table chewed rhythmically on a cheroot, his eyes on Morrison when they were not studying the cards. The hayseeds were soaking up a regular supply of whiskies but Morrison noted that neither of the other two was drinking. He also noted that they were steadily winning. Although neither addressed so much as a word to the other except for the bare requirements of the game, Morrison soon formed the impression that they were working as a team, with the younger of the two, in particular, setting up situations from which the other could profit. The hayseeds were getting plenty of action, but they were steadily being milked. Morrison played his own game, taking care not to tangle seriously with the other two. As time passed it became apparent that they, in return, had marked him out as a solid player, so a tacit conspiracy developed between the three of them to concentrate their energy on depriving the amateurs of the remainder of their cash.

Morrison was making good progress when, around midnight, the younger of the two co-conspirators was forced to take exception to the way Zeke was dealing.

'Sure wish you'd hold them cards down when you're sliding them across the table, mister. Makes it kind of easy for your cronies to see what you're dealing me.'

Zeke stared at him glassily for a moment. He had drunk so much he was doing well even to keep the cards on the table.

'Whad did ya just say, mister?'

'I said, I'd appreciate it if you'd keep my cards confidential,' said the young man in a level voice.

'You ornery sonofagun,' slurred Zeke, stumbling up from his chair. 'You accusing me of cheating? You've already lifted most of my pay off me.'

The older player leant forward, shot a warning glance at the other, and spoke in emollient tones.

'Sit down, *hombre*. The gentleman was criticizing your dealing not your morals.'

'The hell I will!'

Zeke unholstered his six-shooter and waved it unsteadily across the table.

'Guess we'd best settle this outside, mister, Get your hide up off your chair.'

The saloon had suddenly gone quiet as the other patrons became aware that a showdown was in prospect.

Now it was Morrison's turn to lean forward, carefully keeping his hands above the table.

'Don't risk it, boy,' he urged. 'You ain't in no fit state to fight anyone. Put your gun away and don't take things so personal.'

'The hell I will, mister,' Zeke shouted aggressively. 'This stinking trail-louse just called me a cheat.'

He turned back towards his critic. 'You coming outside or not?'

The man made no attempt to move, staring him coolly in the eyes as he replied, 'You just received some good advice, boy. Why not take it?'

'The hell I will, ya no-good, sassy-mouthed yellow-belly.'

Zeke raised his gun, tightening his finger on the trigger. Before his target could make any move to defend himself there was a flash of fire and a deafening report as Chuck Morrison drew his Colt left-handed and spat flame over the green baize. The next moment Zeke's gun was skee-tering uselessly across the sawdust and the boy was clutch-ing in agony at his right wrist.

'Sorry to do that to you, son, but you were about to get yourself killed. Guess a sore arm's better than six foot of earth up Boot Hill.'

There was silence for a moment as the smoke cleared, and then one of the other hayseeds got unsteadily to his feet.

'Come on, Zeke,' he said, glancing nervously across at Morrison, who had drawn without even standing up from the table. 'Guess we've had enough anyway.'

The hayseeds pocketed their remaining cash and stum-bled out disconsolately, while the noise in the saloon got back to normal.

The older card player across the table nodded to Morrison in acknowledgment of his service. 'Obliged to you, mister. That was real fancy shooting with your left hand. Or are you a natural *zurdo*?'

Morrison held up his bandaged right hand.

'Nope. But I've trained myself for all eventualities.'

'Fancy a drink? I guess we owe you one.'

'Thanks. Whiskey.'

The three of them sat counting their winnings. The hayseeds had been well and truly milked.

'Guess we can risk a drink, now,' said Morrison with a conspiratorial wink at the other two as he pocketed a profit of nearly fifty dollars.

The younger man chuckled and riffled the deck of cards.

'Like taking candy from a baby, mister. Say, we never did get your name.'

'Chuck Morrison.'

'Glad to know you, Chuck. I'm Seth and this here's my brother Abe.'

The drinks arrived and they raised their glasses.

'You two boys work well together at the table,' remarked Morrison.

'You noticed, huh?' Abe Lancing grinned. 'I appreciate the compliment. But you did pretty well yourself. 'Maybe we should make it a threesome. We could really clean up.'

'Maybe,' said Morrison, non-committally.

'You a stranger round here like us?'

'Just got in this afternoon.'

'Got anywhere to stay?'

'Not yet. What about you?'

'Rode in this afternoon. Got ourselves a cheap room round the back aways.' Abe Lancing studied Morrison for a moment as though trying to decide how far he ought to allow the exchange of information to continue. Then he asked, 'Where are you from, mister?'

'Near Three Rocks.'

Seth Lancing abruptly stopped riffling the cards.

'Kind of quiet round there, isn't it?'

Morrison nodded.

'Usually. Though we had a bit of action yesterday. Homesteader's wife got raped and murdered. Her boy fetched up at the ranch where I was working. That's how we heard.'

'That so?'

Both the Lancings were now sitting rigidly in their chairs paying careful attention to what Morrison had to say.

'Have another drink on us, mister,' said Abe after a moment's silence. 'The night's kind of young. . . .'

'Where in tarnation have you all been, Pa? It's nearly sundown. I've been worried sick all day.'

Jack Ellwood shook his head wearily. 'It was worse than expected, Kathy. They got Jess Riley too.'

'Land sakes, that poor boy.'

'How is he?'

'Spent most of the day sleeping. He's in the spare room.'

'Guess he's about to have company. This is Hank Sefton, Wilma's brother out here on a visit. I said he could bunk down here till we get this sorted out.'

Sefton took off his hat. 'Glad to make your acquaintance Miss Ellwood.'

'Likewise, I'm sure. But I'm real sorry it had to be in these circumstances.'

Sefton bit his lip. The activity of the day had taken his mind off the full extent of the tragedy but now it was hitting him in the belly like a mule kick.

'We'll have some supper later, Hank,' said Ellwood. 'But I guess you'd like to see the boy on your own. You and he have got some serious talking to do.'

When Hank went into the bedroom, Cal Riley was lying on the patchwork quilt dressed in some old clothes of her brother's that Kathy had ferreted out of a store chest. It was five or six years since he'd last seen the boy, and his resemblance to Wilma – especially the thatch of corn-coloured hair – came as a shock.

Sefton sat down on an oak chair near the foot of the bed.

'Hallo, Cal. Do you remember me?'

The boy stared at him in puzzlement 'No, sir.'

'Can't say I'm surprised. I haven't clapped eyes on you since you were a toddler. I'm your Uncle Hank. Your mother's younger brother.'

Cal nodded gravely. 'I remember your name. Ma said you was coming to see us. She was expecting you.'

'I know. I'm sorry I didn't come sooner.'

Sefton paused in embarrassment not knowing how to start. There seemed to be too much distance between the two of them so he stood up, moved round the side of the bed and sat down beside the boy.

'Cal, there's something I've got to say to you.'

'I know about Ma, if that's what you mean.'

Sefton shook his head.

'It's more than that. I'm afraid they got your pa, too. I found him out on the trail this morning.'

He'd expected a flood of tears but the boy seemed to take the news calmly, almost matter-of-factly – as if he'd already anticipated it. Maybe the shock of what had happened to his mother had numbed him to anything else. If so, no matter. Sefton stayed and talked with him a while and then left him to sleep.

'What's the next move, Pa?' asked Kathy an hour or so later, as she ladled out the beef stew that she'd had on and off the stove since late afternoon.

'Westlake's going to send a few wires to all the places within thirty miles where they might have landed up. Soon as he gets a lead he'll organize a posse.'

'I guess you'll be part of it, Mr Sefton?' asked Kathy, filling his plate. 'You sure look like the right type of man for the job.'

Sefton blushed. Pretty young ladies were a rare phenomenon on the cattle trail – and compliments, from whatever source, even rarer. Now that he looked more closely Miss Kathy was very pretty indeed and couldn't have been more than seventeen or eighteen. A good housekeeper for her widowed father, too, by the look of it.

'It's a matter of family duty now, ma'am. I thought I was making a social visit to my sister and her family . . . and instead I find . . . all this. I'm not going back until this business is settled.'

'I'm sorry we can't ride with you, Hank,' said Ellwood. 'But I've got a ranch to run. Anyway, you're sure welcome to hitch your wagon here till it's all over. And the boy, of course. He'll be safe enough here.'

'Talking of running the ranch, Pa,' said Kathy, 'I've got some news for you. Chuck Morrison quit this morning. Seems he had a showdown with Gus Donovan and came off the worse.'

'Did he now?' chuckled Ellwood. 'Can't say I'm surprised. Well, young Gus's been well groomed for the job, so it's no problem, even if he is only twenty-four.'

He turned his gaze down the table to where his two sons were silently wolfing their stew.

'Guess you boys aren't going to find your Friday nights so agreeable from now on. I hear Gus doesn't take too kindly to saloon life. That's why he's got money in the Cattleman's Bank.'

Pat looked up from his stew. 'Oh come on, Pa. We don't need no chaperoning anyways. We're grown up. Leastways, I am. An' Mike'll be eighteen next year.'

'Son, I wouldn't trust you to stay sober at a school-marm's spelling bee. Either Gus goes with you or you don't go at all.'

'Yes, Pa.'

Pat exchanged sulky looks with his younger brother.

'Still, it won't be the same without Chuck,' he mumbled to nobody in particular.

'Reckon I might be ready for a little business now.'

Chuck Morrison smiled cautiously at Belle Dunnett. He had left the Lancings at the card table finishing their drinks. They had been sympathetic listeners to his tale of ill-treatment at the hands of Jack Ellwood and Gus Donovan, but even through his wretchedness he had sensed that there was some unspoken motive for their interest in him and he was too tired to sit around while they indulged in a lot of verbal fencing.

'Glad to see you took my advice, cowboy. I saw you win a few pots off them hicks. Care to spend your winnings?'

'I might consider it.'

Belle Dunnett put her hand on his arm and led him round to a quieter corner of the bar. It was difficult to discuss business with the smoke and clatter of the saloon at full pitch around them. 'How much you willing to invest in a good time then?'

Chuck Morrison took a moment to consider. Belle's scent was powerfully alluring and her low-cut dress was leaving little to his imagination. His hands were already sweating in anticipation of getting hold of what he could see down there. But as Belle whispered the tariff to him he was forced to scale down his ambitions: he hadn't won that much tonight. So a few minutes later the two of them were out back behind the kitchen door and Belle was getting to work with practised hands. After they had finished he buttoned himself up and made up the alley towards main street. He'd almost reached the corner when two men stepped out of the shadows and barred his path.

'Just a minute, mister. We want a word with you.'

It was too dark to make out faces, but he recognized the voice as that of Al from the poker game.

'Who's we?'

'Me and Carl here. We didn't take too kindly to the way you shot Zeke. It wasn't friendly.'

'I saved him from getting killed, boy. Ain't that friendly enough for you?'

Al made no reply. Instead, he lowered his head and butted Morrison heavily in the chest, following it up with his knee in Morrison's groin. Morrison went down like a ninepin as Carl landed a kick in his kidneys with the point of his boot. Morrison yelled with pain and rolled over in the mud in an effort to protect himself from further assault.

Then he heard a familiar voice.

'Now come on, boys, two on to one just isn't fair.'

Abe Lancing put his hand on Al's shoulder, spun him round and landed his gloved fist square in his mouth. As the youngster spat out a handful of teeth Seth unholstered his sidearm, gripped it by the muzzle and whipped it with demonic fury across Carl's head. It was all over within seconds. The Lancings booted the two boys the length of the alley and watched them scuttle off behind some warehouses. Morrison was struggling to his feet as they walked back to him.

'Thanks, boys. I guess you returned me a favour.'

'Lucky we was just heading back to our boarding-house when we heard the shindig. You'd better keep us company, mister.'

Abe glanced at the knuckle of his glove, grimaced with disgust, and flicked away one of Al's teeth which had embedded itself in the leather. He paused in the light of an oil lamp that was hanging over the boardwalk and leered at Morrison.

'There's safety in numbers. . . . And anyway, we've been talking things over and we've got a proposition we want to put to you. . . .'

*

Hank Sefton had stripped to his longjohns and was about to turn down the lamp when he became aware that Cal still had his eyes open.

'You still awake, boy? It's past midnight.'

Sefton extinguished the light and slid into the bed he was to share with his nephew.

'Guess I couldn't sleep, sir.'

'Not surprising,' Hank grunted.

Sefton lay back staring into the gloom above his head. His own mind was churning away too.

So much to think of and nothing clear at all.

'Uncle Hank, Mom said you've been on some real big cattle drives. Is that true?'

'True enough.'

'That's what I'd like to do. How old was you when you started?'

'About fifteen.'

'Couple of years I'll be that age.'

'That so?'

Hank lay there with his own thoughts while the boy plied him with questions – intelligent ones at that – about life on the trail. He answered mechanically for a while and then decided to call a halt. He had a long day behind him and a long day ahead most likely.

'That's enough questions for tonight. Time you were asleep.'

'Yessir.'

He noted the contented sigh Cal heaved as he curled up and slipped into almost immediate sleep. Maybe, despite everything, it would all turn out right.

SEVEN

Sefton slept as deeply as his nephew, but when the breakfast horn woke him sharp enough at six o'clock he was ready and eager for the day. Warm sunlight was already pouring into the bedroom through the thin muslin curtains, He rolled over and studied his nephew for a moment. Cal was sleeping on blissfully, undisturbed by the horn or the noises of boots on tiles and horses nickering as the ranch came to life.

Sefton got quietly out of bed and dressed himself, making sure not to disturb the boy. Cal would be all the fitter for a quiet day, and there was no point in having him underfoot. Sefton had his breakfast, exchanged a few words with Jack Ellwood about his plans, and went out in search of Gus Donovan, whom he'd met briefly the previous evening.

'Howdy,' said Donovan, when Sefton ran him to earth outside the bunkhouse.

'Fine morning,' acknowledged Sefton. Then studied Donovan for a moment. Last night it had been too dark to get a proper look at him but now Sefton approved of what he saw. Donovan was about his own age, although a bit taller, and well muscled under his check shirt. His face was tanned and frank-looking under a mop of thick black hair.

'I'll be needing my horse,' said Sefton. 'Got some riding to do.'

'Sure.'

Donovan looked around and beckoned to a fresh-faced boy of about fifteen who was filling the drinking trough by the corral.

'Tom, over here.'

Tom Phillips, the youngest of Ellwood's hands, came running up at Donovan's command.

'Yessir?'

'Saddle up Mr Sefton's horse. It's the pinto.'

'Right away, Mr Donovan.'

As the boy made off, Donovan gave Sefton a sympathetic look.

'Sure was sorry to hear what happened to your sister – and to Jess. They were real nice people.'

'Thanks. I thought I'd ride over and take a look at that homestead first thing. It's going to need taking care of.'

Donovan nodded. 'It's a nice little spread: several hundred acres of good pasture land, plenty of water. Even some timber. Jess was making money out of it. I guess it's Cal's now, isn't it?'

Sefton rubbed his jaw, not having considered the all legal implications of what had happened yesterday. He'd come up here for a sort of vacation, but life was getting more complicated by the minute. He ignored Donovan's question. There wasn't much point in having family business discussed all over the ranch.

'I was kind of hoping you could give me directions to get over there.'

Donovan drew a rudimentary sketch map of the area in the sand with the tip of his boot. When Tom came up a few minutes later with his horse, Sefton mounted up and headed toward the gate. As he did so Mike Ellwood came running around the corner of the house clutching a rifle.

'Just a minute, mister,' said Mike, clutching hold of Rayo's bridle.

'Something wrong?'

Mike Ellwood shook his head. 'No. It's just that I wanted you to have this.' He held out his rifle, a well-kept Winchester.

'But. . . .'

'Take it mister . . . er . . . Hank. I owe you for what you did for me out on the trail yesterday. And you seem kind of naked with only your six-shooters. I figure if you're going to go scrapping with a couple of prairie skunks you might need it. I brought you a box of shells, too.'

'Thanks. I appreciate the offer,' said Sefton, examining the rifle carefully. 'Fine-looking weapon. I'll take good care of it until this business is settled.'

An hour or so later, he was viewing the Riley homestead from the bluffs above the creek. It was much as he remembered it from his last visit over six years ago, except that there was no reassuring wisp of smoke coming from the kitchen chimney and no Wilma standing with welcoming arms at the gate as he'd imagined it in his journey up from Yuma.

He took an hour or so to check around. Sooner or later, of course, he would have to bring Cal back here, but he needed to make sure there were no tell-tale signs of the violence that had occurred two nights ago.

The sheriff's men had done a good job. The bedroom and kitchen had been tidied and the bodies removed to town. Sefton looked in the barn and the other outhouses and made them as secure as possible. Then he roped up the two horses in the corral and headed off with them towards Three Rocks.

Seth Lancing put his shoulder against the tumble-down cabin door and applied his weight. The door gave way with a creaking of dried-up timbers, releasing a cloud of dust and cobwebs on Seth's head and neck.

'You picked a winner here, mister,' he said in disgust.

Chuck Morrison shrugged. The cabin might be filthy but it was positioned just where they needed to be: off the trail midway between Three Rocks and the Double L ranch. They'd ridden out of Sedona Springs before first light so as to be here well before the heat of midday. Whatever misgivings he'd originally had about joining up with a pair of no-goods like the Lancings had been overcome by the promise of a third share in the haul of banknotes that they presumed lay hidden somewhere on the Riley spread. He figured that a thousand bucks would be fair compensation for the years of toil at Jack Ellwood's place and might just be enough to give a fresh start on a spread of his own somewhere. Anyway, he didn't have much to lose.

The cabin was part of a set of disused silver-mine workings abandoned when they found better lodes over in Nevada territory. It would provide enough shelter and privacy. There was even a small stream trickling through the workings, where the miners had tried their hands at panning without much success.

'Make yourselves comfortable, boys. It's going to be a long day.'

They sat down and reviewed their plans. The key to the puzzle was the boy, of course. They thought they knew where he was, but they didn't know what he'd had time to tell, or what anyone else had had time to do.

'Don't see any problem,' Seth Lancing mused as he used a freshly soaked bandanna to clean away some of the congealed blood around the wound in his thigh. He turned his smirking face towards Morrison. 'You take us to the boy and we make him talk. Easy.'

'Maybe,' agreed Morrison. 'But let's not get ahead of

ourselves. If he's told the law about the money then it's already locked up in Matt Westlake's office. The boy's no use to us at all.'

'Don't see why not,' Seth persisted. 'Damn it, it's our money. If worst comes to the worst we can trade the boy for the cash.'

His brother looked at him sceptically.

'Yeah? What's the boy to Westlake? The bank'll be offering a reward for the money but the boy's worth nothing to him.'

'Exactly,' said Morrison. 'So, like we agreed, we check Westlake out first. If the boy hasn't talked then we know what to do. Like as not he stashed the money hoping to use it later.'

There was a brief silence, and then Morrison continued, 'Correction. *I* check out Westlake first. Nobody's going to think anything of me going into Three Rocks.'

'So that means we—'

'So that means,' said Morrison interrupting Seth's laborious train of thought, 'so that means you two cool your heels here till I get back.'

'But—'

Abe Lancing prodded his brother none too gently with the point of his boot.

'But nothing. Chuck's right. Won't do you no harm to rest that leg anyway.'

'All right. . . .' Seth's voice carried no conviction.

'But no tricks, Mr Ex-foreman. Remember that money belongs to me and Abe.'

'Not till you find out where it is,' smiled Morrison equably.

Three Rocks was a two-bit town as Sefton already knew from passing through, but he'd managed to have a busy morning.

First of all he'd taken the horses back to old man Nelson to look after. He had debated whether surrender the pinto, but Rayo had already proved a tough little horse. Once he was convinced that you were going to stick on him he seemed happy to cover the ground without tiring. Having settled the horses, Sefton called at the bank, and then made his way to the sheriff's office. Westlake was leaning back in his armchair with his boots on his desk studying the replies to the wires he'd sent yesterday evening.

'Any news?'

Westlake pulled out a cheroot, struck a vesta on the sole of his boot, lit up and inhaled deeply.

'Maybe. Possible sighting of two likely customers in Sedona Springs last night.'

Sefton straightened his shoulders aggressively.

'Well, what are we waiting for? Let's ride over and check.'

'Hold your fire a minute, Sefton. Just because they were there last night, don't mean to say they'll be there now. As I told you yesterday, I don't want to go riding off on a wild goose chase. In any case we do have a sheriff in Sedona Springs, you know. His name's Kyle Brody and he's almost as good as yours truly. If the Lancings are on his territory he'll want to pick them up as much as you do. Looky here. . . .' Westlake leant forward and picked a poster up from his desk. It was a Wanted notice putting $200 apiece on the Lancings' heads.

'Come on, Sheriff,' protested Sefton. 'We can't just sit here and do nothing. Somebody should be trailing those vermin before they get clear out of the state.'

He started to pace up and down the confines of the cluttered office snapping his fingers with frustration. For the sheriff this was just another matter of routine business, but for Sefton it was personal. He kept the argument going for a time, but Westlake was immovable. He wasn't going to raise a posse until he was sure which way the Lancings were headed. And that was that.

'All right,' said Sefton in disgust, when it became clear that, for the moment at least, Westiake would not be moved, 'I'll see you around, Sheriff.' He turned abruptly on his heel.

'Just a minute, just a minute. Where exactly are you fixing to go?'

'First of all to the saloon for the beer I've been promising myself all morning – then to Sedona Springs, of course.'

'Forget it, Sefton,' snapped Westlake. 'You're in danger of setting yourself up as a one-man lynch party. Stay put till we can sort this out properly.'

'Sorry, Sheriff. This is family business and I don't intend to sit around doing nothing.'

'You're crazy and I'm not about to let you make a fool of yourself.'

'How are you going to stop me? By putting me behind bars again?'

Without giving Westlake the opportunity to reply, Sefton slammed out of the office and headed up to the saloon. Thrusting his way impatiently through the batwing doors he saw that it was deserted except for a solitary customer leaning against the bar. The figure turned round on hearing the doors clatter, and then straightened perceptibly as Sefton approached.

'Step right up, mister,' said Chuck Morrison.

Sefton hesitated for a moment and then positioned himself at the other end of the bar.

Morrison grinned as he noted the strategic distance Sefton had maintained.

'No need to be shy, mister. I ain't looking for revenge. I'll even let you buy me a drink.'

Sefton studied the bandage on Morrison's hand for a moment, shrugged and moved closer.

'Beer?' asked Lou, as Sefton leant against the bar.

'Yeah.' Sefton nodded towards Morrison. 'Set one up for him too.'

'Appreciate it mister. Kind of down on my luck at the moment.'

'So I heard.'

Sefton would have been happy to concentrate on his drink, but Morrison was intent on conversation.

'Sorry to hear about your sister. She was a real fine woman. If I'd known who you were I wouldn't have picked a quarrel the other night. I was only doing it to save Pat and Mike some money. Then their old man kicks me out for my pains.'

Sefton decided to accept the peace offering. 'That's all right. Looks like you got a raw deal all round.'

'Any chance of getting the critters that done it?'

'Sheriff's working on it. Reckons he knows who they are, anyway. Lancing brothers – already wanted for a bank job down in Halesville.'

Morrison affected a whistle of surprise.

'That one? I heard tell they made away with three thousand bucks.'

'Apparently. Makes it kind of easy for them to get away, doesn't it?'

As Sefton frowned into his half-empty glass Morrison relaxed perceptibly, fairly certain from the tone of Sefton's voice that he wasn't bluffing and that he knew nothing about what the boy had done with the money.

'You staying in town now, mister?'

'No, Jack Ellwood's given me and the boy a room. I guess it's the best place at the moment.'

'Sure thing,' said Morrison, downing the remains of his drink. 'Safest place too, I guess.'

The conversation continued in a desultory way for a few minutes until Sefton drained his second beer, tossed a few coins on the bar in settlement and walked out. He made his way to the livery stables, collected Rayo and checked on the route to Sedona Springs. It would be an easy ride: there was a well-beaten stagecoach trail from Three Rocks which would be simple to follow.

Scarcely a quarter of a mile out of town, however, Sefton was forced into an abrupt change of plans. Hearing the sound of hoofbeats coming up fast behind him he turned in his saddle to find Westlake bearing down on him.

'What now, Sheriff?' he asked, as Westlake drew level. 'You arresting me for being a disobedient boy?'

'Forget the humour, Sefton. If you insist on getting yourself killed I'm not going to stop you. But I just got a piece of information that I thought it only polite to share before you were quite out of my jurisdiction.'

'Namely?'

'Kyle Brody just wired through. Seems that the Lancings lit out of Sedona early this morning with one other person unknown. If that's where you're headed, you're wasting your time.'

Sefton bit his lip in frustration. 'Seems I'm getting nowhere fast.'

He stared longingly at the trail leading across the distant hills towards Sedona Springs, hesitated, and then reluctantly turned back for Three Rocks with Westlake. Later that evening he arrived at the Double L – deflated, dejected, but not, as he took pains to emphasize to an attentive Miss Kathy, defeated. . . .

It was a full moon, which made their task easier; that, and the fact that the ranch dogs knew Morrison. Without him they could never have got within a hundred yards of the ranch house without provoking a cacophony of barking and chain rattling.

They approached the entrance to the Double L ranch well after midnight. Morrison knew every inch of the terrain, of course: he'd been riding it for close on fifteen years. Even so, the full moon was a help. They let Morrison go on ahead. The dogs had to be silenced and he was the only one who could do it. Jack Ellwood kept two: one chained by the entrance to the ranch and one in a kennel round the back of the ranch house by the kitchen door.

Morrison had taught the dogs to recognize him by using a special low whistle. It was especially helpful when he and the boys came back late on Friday nights and didn't want to wake up the whole house. So the first dog made no sound when Morrison approached, softly whistling as usual. It simply trotted out to the end of its chain wagging its tail in anticipation as Morrison bent over it and stove in its skull with the club he'd brought for the purpose.

He beckoned to the others and they walked their horses in towards the house as far as they dared without risking any noise. Now he had to repeat the operation with the other dog. He edged round the side of the house and approached as close as he could to the kitchen door before beginning to whistle. Once again the ruse worked and the second dog was despatched as ruthlessly as the first. Now he and Abe could get down to business, while Seth held the horses ready for a smart getaway.

There was a large storage shed among the outbuildings to the rear of the house. Treading cautiously in the moonlight, Morrison led Abe over and carefully eased open the door. There was only the faintest trace of moonlight shining in through the open door, and the rest of the interior was inky black. It didn't matter though: Morrison knew exactly what he was looking for – in fact he'd stored it there himself quite recently.

All the way down the left-hand wall were wooden shelves stacked with paint, creosote, varnishes and oils. About halfway along, Morrison eased out a small drum of turpentine which they carefully rolled outside. They manhandled it across the yard to the bunkhouse and unscrewed the stopper. Morrison paused to listen before moving to the final stage of the plan. There was no sound from inside apart from the occasional snore.

Now they worked their way methodically round the bunkhouse sprinkling turpentine all along the boards at the base of the structure. When they'd made a complete circuit and the drum was empty Morrison nodded to his companion. Abe made his way back to the front of the house and waited.

With a grin of satisfaction at what he hoped he was about to achieve, Morrison stepped back, extracted a match from the pocket of his pants, struck it and hurled it into a pool of turpentine by the bunkhouse door. Then he retreated to a corner of the house to watch developments.

The turpentine ignited immediately, producing an almost instantaneous ring of flame right round the wooden bunkhouse. It took a few minutes, however, for the timbers to really catch fire, and a further few minutes for the occupants inside to become aware of the smoke and flames with which they were surrounded. When the reality of their situation became apparent, all hell broke loose.

The walls of the bunkhouse were flaring up in sparks and crackles, and the doorway was engulfed in flames. Those cowboys who were sleeping nearest the door rushed out relatively unscathed and raised the alarm. This woke the whole household and brought everyone out to see what was going on. The yells of terror from those inside the bunkhouse who now found the doorframe a ring of fire added to the pandemonium.

Hank Sefton had found sleep elusive. He'd bunked down with the rest of the Ellwood household by 10.30, but he lay awake wondering whether he had done the right thing in not pressing on to Sedona Springs by himself that afternoon. Cal had already gone to bed by the time he got back to the ranch. Sefton envied the ease with which his nephew managed to forget his troubles in sleep. He wondered how effectively he was discharging his duties towards Cal not only as his uncle, but also his guardian. He'd scarcely spoken to the boy today. It had been a long day in Three Rocks, but somehow not a very productive one. Cal, on the other hand, seemed to have done better. When he had eventually woken up he had apparently spent the day trailing young Tom Phillips and helping with the various tasks assigned by Gus Donovan. Kathy Ellwood reported that the boy was so enthusiastic about life on a big ranch that he'd even pleaded to eat his evening chow with the rest of the hands at the *parrilla* outside the cook-house instead of sitting down with the family.

Sefton had only just fallen into an uneasy sleep when he became aware of the disturbance outside. The window of his bedroom was at the side of the house, but the reflected glare of the flames as the bunkhouse caught fire was quite discernible when he raised the curtain and peered out into the night. Without stopping to pull on boots or pants he rushed out in his underwear down the passage and through the kitchen – with Jack Ellwood close behind him muttering baffled curses. The bunkhouse was well alight by now and a group of hands who'd been lucky enough to make their escape early were huddled round in their underwear waiting for someone to take charge.

Jack Ellwood took in the situation at a glance and could see that there was no way of saving the bunkhouse even if they had a supply of water close by. He elbowed his way roughly through the crowd.

'Anyone else still in there?'

'We ain't seen Gus, Mr Ellwood. He was sleeping down the far end.'

With an oath Ellwood turned to his sons who were standing behind him rubbing their eyes in disbelief.

'Pat, get that heavy Indian rug from the passage.'

The flames were licking as high as the bunkhouse roof now and it was apparent that the building didn't have much longer to stand. When Pat emerged from the kitchen dragging the rug, Ellwood grabbed it, ran over to the drinking trough and soused it with water. Then he draped it over his head and dived in through the flaming doorway. There was a terrible minute during which all they could hear was the hiss and crackle of burning timber and then Ellwood emerged with not one, but two other figures. Beside him, sheltering under the smouldering rug was Gus Donovan: in his arms was the slender frame of Tom Phillips.

They tumbled out and collapsed coughing and choking on the ground as the bunkhouse erupted in a wall of flame and the roof and walls caved in.

'Pa, Pa, are you all right?' screamed Kathy.

'Let's get them inside,' ordered Sefton. 'Somebody light the lamps in the kitchen.'

'I'm all right,' spluttered Ellwood through a spasm of coughing. 'I just took down a lot of smoke. See to Gus and the boy.'

Gus Donovan seemed to be flat out, but they carried him inside and managed to bring him round. He'd obviously taken in lungfuls of smoke and was going to spend the night retching, but didn't seem to have been seriously burnt. Tom Phillips, who had apparently passed out in the bunkhouse, was also revived but his groans indicated worse damage. When they eased him on to his side they saw that his underclothing was scorched where one of the rafter beams had fallen close by, scattering sparks over him.

'This is a job for me, Pa,' said Kathy decisively. 'We'll have to cut his clothes away. Mr Sefton would you mind getting my work basket? It's in the chest in your room. Top drawer. I need my pinking shears.'

As Sefton hurried off she added, 'Looks like someone was careless with a cheroot tonight.'

'That wasn't a careless cheroot, Miss Kathy,' coughed Donovan. 'The flames were coming from the outside. Someone did this deliberate.'

'The hell they did,' agreed Ellwood. He gazed around at the others. 'And I haven't heard a dog bark.'

Before he could say anything else there was a thumping of bare feet and a distraught Sefton appeared in the doorway.

'It's Cal,' he gasped. 'He's gone.'

EIGHT

Cal Riley's dreams had suddenly become threatening. He was in a shipwreck and the waters were closing over his head. He was thrashing about in the water but to no avail. Now he was sinking and there was no way to breathe.

His eyes opened as he struggled into consciousness to realize that he really was thrashing about and that he was close to suffocating. A horny hand was pressed tight around his mouth while another was forcing one of his arms behind his back and lifting him painfully out of his bed. Unable to yell, he swivelled his eyes frantically to left and right trying to make out who was manhandling him. Surely it wasn't Uncle Hank. The room was dark apart from a strange orange glow at the window, and he could make out nothing but a pair of vague shadows with him in the room. One of them had him in a vice-like grip now, and the other was dragging the patchwork quilt off the bed.

The pressure on his mouth lifted for a moment, but immediately a kerchief or bandanna was stuffed in between his teeth and knotted tight behind his neck. Then he found himself being rolled up in the quilt. Thus immobilized and silenced, he was carried swiftly and silently out of the house.

The next hour or so was a blur as he floated in and out

of terrified consciousness. He was aware of being slung face down over a horse, and of a subsequent hard gallop over rough terrain with the pommel jarring painfully into his ribs and every jolt shaking the breath out of his body. The gag had not been removed and he had to concentrate all his conscious efforts on controlling his breathing through his nose. Towards the end of the ride he must have passed out, because when he next became aware of anything he was propped up against a wall somewhere with a man bending over him untying the gag.

'Told you it was too tight. If you've gone and suffocated him I'm gonna blow your brains out.'

Cal recognized the voice as that of Abe Lancing and understood immediately what had happened and whose hands he was in.

'Get that scorpion out of your pants, Brother. He's still breathing, all right. Just a little winded maybe, but we can soon fix that.'

Cal shivered when he recognized the voice of Seth Lancing. There followed an agonizing moment of suspense until Seth's hand descended hard across his face. Cal yelled in surprise and terror.

'There you are, Brother! I told you he was all right.'

Forcing himself to focus his eyes through his pain Cal tried to make out something of his surroundings. He seemed to be in a small wooden shack lit only by the inadequate gleam of three or four tallow candles. Abe Lancing was standing in front of him, with another man he didn't recognize. Seth was still bending over him with his hand forced hard underneath his chin holding his head up and rigid. Cal flinched in expectation of another blow and tried to turn his head but Seth's grip was too strong.

'He's still got his voice, you see.' Seth chuckled. 'That's all we need. You got anything to say for yourself now, boy?'

'Please, mister, I'll do what you want. Don't make my nose bleed again.'

Cal's voice came out as a croak. Seth relaxed his grip.

'That's real sensible, boy, because you're in a mighty big heap of trouble.'

Cal relaxed trembling against the wall. He was still rolled in the quilt and it seemed as though a rope had been drawn tightly around it, because he couldn't move his arms.

'You know what you are, boy?' Seth continued.

'No, mister.'

'You're a thief. A dirty little skunk-tailed thief. You know why?'

'I took your money, mister.'

Cal started to snivel. Seth's use of the word *thief* had suddenly jogged his conscience. He'd rifled the saddle-bags as a means of revenge for what he'd been forced to listen to as the Lancings exercised their animal instincts on his mother. But it was his mother who had told him many times that two wrongs didn't make a right. He knew he should have said what he'd done back at the Double L ranch, but to begin with he'd been expecting to have his father to confess to, and then he hadn't been quite sure of his Uncle Hank. And yesterday there hadn't really been any opportunity to talk to him. So now it looked as though he was really going to pay the price for what he'd done.

'Glad you know you done wrong, boy,' remarked Seth, noting his tears with satisfaction. 'You put us to a real load of inconvenience. That weren't at all considerate.'

Cal flinched as Seth's arm swung back again, but the third man took a pace forward and intervened.

'That's enough, Seth. He's only a kid. Pick on someone your own size. Besides, he's here for a reason. Remember?'

Chuck Morrison shoved Seth roughly to one side,

grabbed hold of Cal inside his quilt, lifted him up and propped him on a wooden bench further along the wall.

'Take it easy, son. You're smart enough to know what we want.'

'Yes, mister.'

'Then you know you've got a choice. You either tell us where the money is, or we make you tell us. Which do you want?'

'I'll tell you, mister. I didn't mean no harm.'

'All right. Start talking and don't waste no more of our time. . . .'

'He's gone all right, Pa.'

Pat Ellwood, properly dressed now, shrugged his shoulders as he stood in front of his father in the living-room of the ranch. They'd poked some life back into the log fire which was now crackling in the stone hearth, and Kathy was in the kitchen making coffee. Pat and Sefton had gone through the motions of searching the ranch, but it was clear that Cal had been taken. Bit by bit they pieced together the sequence of events, but a complete explanation for what had happened still eluded them.

'It was Chuck who got them in here,' remarked Mike disconsolately. 'Nobody else could have got past them two dogs – not even Apaches. He's cost us two good watchdogs.'

'And a bunkhouse, goddam him,' growled Ellwood senior. 'It was well thought out,' he acknowledged with grudging admiration. 'They couldn't have been in here more than a couple of minutes, and there was so much racket going on outside that nobody could possibly have heard them come or go.'

Hank Sefton sat silently on a stool by the hearth with his head in his hands. Just before going to sleep he'd been reproaching himself for not doing enough to protect Cal's interests. Now the boy had been snatched almost from under his very eyes. Some uncle, some guardian! His first instinct when it became clear the boy had gone was to rush out in his underpants in wild pursuit. But Jack Ellwood had soon persuaded him that even properly dressed, on horseback, it would be pointless. You couldn't go chasing off in the dark when you hadn't the least idea where your quarry was headed.

'I guess some of this is my fault, Mr Ellwood.'

Gus Donovan had recovered his normal breathing, and apart from feeling as though his scorched lungs were caked with soot, he knew he was going to be all right.

'I mean, Chuck was really getting his own back for what I did to him the other morning. If they wanted a diversion they could've set fire to one of the outhouses without risking any lives.'

'Don't blame yourself, Gus. Chuck couldn't have thought this one up on his own. He had help.'

'I still don't get it,' said Hank, scratching his head. 'What do they want with Cal?'

'Maybe somebody's scared he's the only witness to what they did to your sister, in which case we know who they are.'

'In that case why didn't they just kill him? It doesn't make sense. And if they've already got three thousand bucks they can hardly be thinking of holding him to ransom when they've already done for both his parents.'

A faint voice intruded into the conversation from the corner.

'But that's the point, Mr Sefton, they ain't got three thousand bucks.'

All eyes turned towards the settle where they had deposited Tom Phillips. The boy had levered himself painfully on to his side. His breathing was better, but he wouldn't relish sitting on a horse for a good few days.

Sefton frowned in puzzlement. 'But that's what Sheriff Westlake said they got away with.'

'Yessir. But I don't think they've got it with them now.'

Jack Ellwood stood up and walked across to the boy.

'Son, will you just explain what in tarnation you're talking about. Or has all that smoke got into your brain as well as your lungs?'

'Honest, Mr Ellwood, I'm trying to talk sense. It's just that yesterday when me and Cal was working together and talking about what happened at the Riley place he said that he'd outsmarted them twice – by escaping and making sure they wouldn't enjoy their loot.'

Hank joined Ellwood by the settle and crouched down beside Phillips.

'What did he mean *wouldn't enjoy their loot?*'

'He wouldn't explain, sir. But he said he was going to talk to you about it later.'

'Which he didn't, because I was late back here,' said Hank disgustedly.

'Sounds to me,' said Ellwood, 'as if he could have made off with the money himself – and they never found out till too late. After all, he had the opportunity. He said they were both curled up like hibernating polecats when he lit out of there.'

'So where did he put it?' asked Pat. 'It wasn't with him when he came stumbling in here that morning.'

'Kind of obvious, isn't it?' said his brother. 'It's still on the farm. A kid like Cal would know exactly where to hide it. He's smart enough.'

Jack Ellwood looked across at his son approvingly.

'Mike, that's the first time I've heard you talk sense in months. Guess you really are growing up.'

Cal Riley peered uneasily about him in the gloom that was only faintly relieved by the flickering candles. The guttering flames created grotesque leering distortions on his captors' faces as they peered down at him. He shivered, despite the quilt. He only had his underwear beneath it, and the splintered boards under his bare feet felt icy cold. Despite his tiredness and confusion at having been woken out of a deep sleep he forced himself to try and keep his wits about him.

'Now listen carefully, boy,' Chuck Morrison was saying. 'I'm gonna ask you some questions and I want straight answers with no hesitation. If I catch you wasting my time I'm handing you over to my friend here.'

He paused dramatically to indicate the shadowy figure of Seth by his shoulder.

'I guess you already found out he don't mind teaching boys their manners. You understand me?'

'Yes, mister,' whispered Cal.

'All right. Did you take their money?'

'Yes, mister.'

'Where did you hide it?'

'On my dad's farm, mister.'

'Have you told anyone else about it?'

Cal had managed to anticipate this question. He assumed the most innocent look he could muster before he replied. Then he looked Morrison straight in the face. 'Mister, I swear I haven't told nobody where the money is. You know I never had a chance to tell my pa.'

'And you never told Ellwood?'

'On my honour, mister, I never told him. Nobody knows where it is except me.'

Cal sensed all three of the men exhaling with satisfaction in the gloom.

'All right. Now tell me. *Where's the money hid?*'

Despite his exhaustion Cal was alert enough to realize that the answer to this question would decide whether he lived or died here and now. Once the men knew exactly where the money was they had no further use for him. Equally, if they suspected he was stalling them he could reckon on Seth beating the information out of him with no compunction. He had to sound plausible.

'I buried it, mister.'

'Where did you bury it?'

'Under the barn floor.'

'That ain't no use to us, boy,' snarled Abe. 'That barn's bigger than a house.'

'I know, mister, that's why I picked it,' said Cal. 'I can't explain exactly which part out of my head. But I sure could show you.' He tried to sound eager – as if he really wanted to help them.

'I think he's a lying little rattlesnake,' said Seth, quietly. 'He knows danged well where he put those bills and he's just stalling us. Give him here to me. I'll soon find out the truth.'

He leant forward and dragged Cal from off the bench, Cal yelped and appealed to Morrison, who he could sense was the only faint ally he had here.

'Please mister, don't let him touch me. I'm trying to help you, I promise.'

'You're a liar,' said Seth, not relaxing his grip. 'Gimme one of those candles, Abe. There's a quick way of sorting this out once and for all.'

'Leave him alone,' said Morrison, sharply. 'I'm willing to take a chance on him. If he's been holding out on us he can pay for it when we get there. In the meantime I don't much reckon with torturing kids.'

'Suit yourself, Mr High and Mighty.' Seth's voice was full of venom. 'Go outside if you don't want to watch. But I'll do as I want and you ain't stopping me.'

'No,' said Morrison, 'but this will.'

The Colt had appeared in his left hand as if by magic, just the way it had in the saloon. Seth stared at the candlelight flickering menacingly on the gunmetal. It was true that there were two of them to take Morrison on, but one of them was certain to get shot in the process – and it was Seth at whom the gun was pointing.

'No need to get excited, Brother,' said Abe. 'I don't see any problem in taking the kid along with us. He knows what he'll get if he's been lying.'

Morrison kept the gun pointed at Seth's belly as he waited for him to back down.

'All right,' Seth said after a tense pause. 'But I don't like it. That kid tricked us twice already. If I'd had my way with him in the first place, none of this would have happened.'

'Looks like you win, mister,' said Abe to Morrison with a rueful grin. 'Now, I suggest we all settle down and get some shut-eye. We've got an early start to make.'

NINE

There was only the merest suspicion of pink in the eastern sky when the Lancings and their prisoner rode away from the cabin. For the next hour or so they were in Morrison's hands as only he knew the quickest and safest way to the Riley spread. Cal Riley had been allowed a few hours' feverish sleep parcelled up in the quilt. Then they had roused him and extracted him from his cocoon. It had been Seth Lancing's pleasure to use the rope that had been tied round the outside of the quilt to bind Cal's hands with ferocious severity behind his back. The boy had nothing but the underwear that he stood up in, so Chuck Morrison draped his leather jacket round his shoulders against the morning cold. He would soon warm up as the sun rose. They harnessed their mounts and set off with Cal perched on the front of Morrison's saddle. Despite the agony of his tightly bound wrists he was at least relieved not to be riding with either of the Lancings. Even so, the ride was bad enough. Apart from Morrison's restraining arm around his middle he had no means of balancing himself against the jolting of the horse, and the rope was steadily chafing his wrists raw. Added to this, his mind was a whirlwind of emotions – one half desperately wanting the journey to end, the other half petrified at the prospect of what was going to happen to him when it did.

97

Morrison led the way at a brisk canter using his years of knowledge of the local ground to pick a secure route. Shortly after dawn they found themselves approaching the summit of the bluffs that overlooked the Riley homestead. Cal's relief at finding himself once more on territory that he recognized, and of which he knew every inch, was tempered with the dread of what was coming next.

Before they headed the bluffs Morrison put up his hand to bring the two others to a halt.

'That's it, gentlemen. Time to do a bit of walking.'

'What in tarnation for?' demanded Seth. 'We know where we are now. Why don't we just ride in and take what we've come for?'

Abe Lancing gave his brother a contemptuous look and dismounted to stand with Morrison.

'You sure ain't much good at thinking ahead, Brother. How do we know what we're going find down there? Somcone at Ellwood's place must have been wondering why we snatched the boy. Suppose they put two and two together and have it staked out?'

'They're not that smart,' said Seth. 'Unless the kid was lying to us when he said he hadn't told nobody. I did point out that possibility last night, but you weren't interested.'

'No point in taking chances,' intervened Morrison before the brotherly conversation could get really acrimonious. 'Besides, the sun's going to be behind us as we top the bluffs. If there's anybody waiting on that spread they'll pick up our outlines easy as pie as we come over the ridge.'

'So we walk,' said Abe to his brother with satisfaction in his voice.

'No,' corrected Morrison. 'We crawl till we can get a view. Leastways, you and me do. Your brother can stay here with the kid and the horses.'

Morrison and Abe Lancing walked up the reverse slope of the ridge and then dropped to their bellies as they neared the top. Using their knees and elbows they wormed their way forward through the grit until they had a clear view of what was down below.

Back with the horses, Cal eyed Seth Lancing nervously. With Morrison dismounted he had been able to settle back properly into the saddle. The temptation simply to dig his bare heels into the horse's flanks and gallop it away was almost overwhelming, but he knew he couldn't risk it. With his hands tied behind his back and his feet unable to reach the stirrups he'd be thrown as soon as the horse started forward. In any case, almost as if he'd read Cal's thoughts Seth made sure of grabbing Morrison's horse by the face strap. There wasn't going to be any easy way out of this one.

Cal looked forlornly down at Seth. 'Please, mister, will you loosen my hands a little? They're hurting real bad.'

'That so?' said Seth with a smirk. 'Mister, that rope ain't coming off till I needs it to throttle you with after we got that money – just like I did to your ma. In any case, if you're hurting now it ain't nothing compared with what you'd feel when the circulation comes back.'

He chuckled contentedly as Cal started to snivel.

Up on the ridge Morrison was wishing he had a pair of binoculars. The sun was just about high enough in the sky to make the Riley spread visible but they weren't close enough to pick up much detail.

'What do you reckon?' he asked Abe Lancing.

'Looks quiet. Seems much as we left it couple of days ago. Except for one thing.'

'What's that?'

'Ain't no horses in the corral. Someone's been there.'

'Well, that isn't surprising if you say you left Riley's body out on the trail.'

They lay there for a full five minutes inspecting the house and every one of the outbuildings.

There was no trace of movement anywhere.

'Looks like we go down, then,' said Morrison.

They inched backwards, only standing up when their heads were safely below the level of the ridge.

'Ghost town, down there,' said Abe to his brother as they reached the horses and mounted up again. This time Morrison let Abe take the lead, unwilling to take the first bullet if in fact there should be anyone out there. They picked their way slowly and quietly down towards the creek, edged their horses over the wooden boards of the little bridge that crossed the water and approached the entrance to the farm. Once inside the spruce log palings they dismounted and tethered their horses to the outside of the corral.

'Gimme the kid,' said Abe to Morrison.

He grabbed Cal by the hair and paraded him in front as they made their way Indian file towards the barn. The boy would be a perfect shield in case of trouble, but the silence, apart from the clucking of a few chickens in a coop somewhere behind the house, was total.

'Right, boy,' muttered Abe, as they approached the barn door, 'this is when we find out whether you were telling the truth.'

He edged the barn door open and pushed Cal inside ahead of him. Seth was following right behind. He paused with his left hand resting on the doorframe to whisper to Morrison, 'Mister, you're about to get rich.'

At the same moment there was a muffled report and the crack of splintering timber as a rifle bullet whacked into the doorframe an inch from Seth's head. For a second he failed to react, and then he screamed in rage and pain as he looked down at the severed middle finger of his left hand where it had dropped at his feet, still in its morsel of shredded glove. Before he could speak, Morrison had shoved him violently in the back and they both pitched headfirst into the shelter of the barn.

*

'Sonofagun, I just can't believe I missed him!'

Hank Sefton stared down in disgust at the Winchester which he'd trained on the barn from the shelter of the farmhouse door. He didn't figure himself much of a sure-shot with hand guns, but give him a rifle and the opportunity of a good steady aim and he reckoned he could nail a sparrow between the eyes at a hundred yards. But not this morning, evidently. He'd had to let Abe Lancing pass because of the risk of hitting the boy, but the other one should have been vulture meat by now.

'Don't take it personal, son,' whispered Jack Ellwood in his ear. 'Judging by the sound he made you must have winged him at least.'

He moved over to the window to see if he could spot any movement at the barn.

'Looks like we guessed right, anyway,' said Ellwood staring through the flimsy curtain.

They'd made their plans in the small hours of the morning on three assumptions. Firstly, that Cal had hidden the money; secondly, that it was on the Riley homestead; and thirdly, that they'd need to be very early risers if they were going to beat the Lancings to it. In fact, they had no guarantee that the Lancings hadn't ridden straight here from the Double L ranch, although they guessed it was unlikely. Before the Lancings committed themselves they'd have to make certain that Cal hadn't stashed the money somewhere on the trail out to Ellwood's – so they'd have to question him first.

They had set off an hour before dawn with the advantage of less distance to cover than the Lancings, and had made their approach just as circumspectly as Chuck Morrison did scarcely an hour later. Once they had established that they had the place to themselves they had time to make their preparations.

Sefton had already realized from his previous visit that the farmhouse was almost impregnable if properly defended – and both he and Ellwood had rifles. It also seemed that the house might be the likeliest place for Cal to have stashed the money – although a quick search had revealed nothing. So, having settled themselves, with their horses well hidden in the trees behind the house, it was just a question of waiting.

That was the worst part of course, but it wasn't long before the three riders and the boy were spotted picking their way down to the creek. By the time they crossed the bridge Hank had opened the door a crack and was down on one knee with the rifle covering the approach to the house. But the Lancings made for the barn instead. Was that where Cal had directed them, then?

'Looks like we've goofed up,' Sefton muttered morosely over his shoulder to Ellwood. 'If I'd taken one of them out it would've shortened the odds in our favour.'

'Take it easy, son,' advised Ellwood. 'Look at it from their point of view. They're holed up in a barn with a rifle trained on the only way out. It's going to get kind of panicky in there as the day gets hotter. Let them sweat a bit. We're a sight more comfortable than they are. And we've got time on our side.'

'Goddammit, mister – don't shut that door. My finger's still outside.'

Seth Lancing stared at his incomplete hand with disbelief as Morrison banged the barn door shut behind them.

'You can pick it up later. It'll still be where you dropped it.'

Seth turned to his brother, pale-faced and almost sobbing with frustration.

'You see what that kid's led us into? I told you he was a lying little rattlesnake. Now you can let me finish him off.'

Abe interposed himself between Cal and his brother before Seth could think of drawing his gun.

'Just hold it a moment, Seth, and cool your butt. We've got some more thinking to do. Chuck, keep an eye on that door and see if you can see what's going on up at the cabin. We've got to know how many we're up against.'

Morrison nodded and crouched against the end wall of the barn with his eye applied to a knothole in the timber, from which he had a reasonable line of vision up to the house. Meanwhile Seth had drawn off his ruined glove and was wrapping a bandanna around the stump of his finger which had been sheared off just above the second knuckle.

'Will you look at this mess,' he groaned as the fabric became saturated with blood.

'Count yourself lucky it wasn't your head. Because that's what he was aiming at – you can bet your bottom dollar.'

Showing no further interest in his brother's recent forcible amputation Abe perched himself calmly on the trestle table with the boy still firmly in his grasp.

'You've got some explaining to do, mister,' he said, shaking Cal's shoulder roughly. 'You said you hadn't told anyone about where you left the money.'

'It's true, mister. I swear I didn't.'

'Then who's the goddam welcoming party? He sure ain't friendly.'

'I don't know, mister,' said Cal, biting his lip. That rifle shot was the best thing he'd heard so far that morning and as far as he was concerned anyone who was willing to shoot Seth's finger off must be a friend. Maybe it was Uncle Hank – but he didn't dare hope too much.

'Can you see anything, Chuck?'

'Nope,' said Morrison, his eye still glued to the knothole.

Seth looked up from nursing his wounded hand and leered sceptically at his brother.

'Well smart-ass, you got any suggestions?'

Abe considered for a moment. 'Maybe we're not so badly off. Remember we've got the boy and we've nearly got the money as well if he's been telling us the truth. Whoever's out there probably wants one or the other or both. Don't see no call to panic.'

'That's right,' said Morrison. 'Except that if it comes to a shoot-out we've got one problem.'

'What's that?'

'We left our rifles with the horses.'

Abe suppressed an oath. Morrison was right, of course. They had just six side-arms between them and only the bullets in their gunbelts. The marksman up in the cabin could keep them pinned down in here effortlessly. Or could he? Well, they could deal with that in a moment. Right now there was surely another priority to sort out.

'All right boy, let's deal with the money. Here's the barn; there's the floor. Now where did you hide it?'

'It's under there, mister,' said Cal, nodding uneasily towards the wall behind them.

'But where, for Moses' sake?' yelled Abe, eyeing at least fifty foot of wall with rising irritation.

'Mister, I . . . I can't tell you from here.'

Abe, on the verge of losing all self control, grabbed him by the hair and jerked his head back.

'Whaddaya mean, you can't tell from here, boy?'

'Mister, I told you the truth when I said it was under the barn floor. I swear it is. But I buried it from outside – that's the only way to find it.'

There was an awful silence for a moment and then Seth, despite his pain, managed a hollow laugh at his brother's visible discomfiture.

'Well isn't that just the cat's whiskers? We're in here and the money's out there.'

'Shut up, damn you,' snarled Abe.

He tightened his grip on Cal's hair till the boy yelled with pain.

'Why didn't you tell us that before, boy?'

'You never gave me a chance, mister. You just marched me straight in here.'

Morrison turned round from his vigil and looked ironically at the Lancings.

'Seems like we're in entirely the wrong place, gentlemen.'

'Thanks to my oh-so-clear-thinking brother here,' said Seth. 'And pinned down in the wrong place.'

'Who said?'

Abe had recovered from his momentary loss of control and was thinking rapidly again. He let go of Cal's hair.

'You got a short memory, Brother. There's another way out of here, remember?' He glanced up at the hayloft. 'Seems to me we can get out any time we like. And if my memory serves me correct we can't be seen from the house.'

There was no time to be lost. Abe shinned up the ladder, made his way across the loft to the opening in the wall and peered through. The outside ladder was still propped against the wall. He craned his neck. To the right he could see the blind end wall of the cabin. But this side of the barn was out of sight of the front of the house. Suddenly they seemed to have gained the initiative.

Abe crawled back inside and made his way down to the others.

'It's OK. We can get out and not be seen from the house.'

'What are we waiting for, then?' asked Morrison.

'Just hold it. Remember we came for the money. We still

ain't got it. Now here's what we'll do. I'll take the boy outside and we'll get the money and bring it back inside. Then—'

'Hold on, hold on,' interrupted his brother. 'Why don't we all come out, get the money and hightail it straight out of here?'

Abe looked despairingly at Morrison.

'Tell him, Chuck.'

Morrison shrugged. 'Maybe he can tell us how we're going to get to our horses. They're plumb in full view of that sharpshooter.'

Abe didn't bother to wait for any reply from his brother. He took hold of Cal's ear and led him towards the ladder.

'Please, mister, untie my hands before we get going. I've got to wriggle down a hole to get that money. I can't do it with my hands tied. Please, mister. They're hurting real bad.'

Abe considered. The boy's pain was irrelevant, but if his hands were tied Abe would be hauling him up and down two ladders – with the added complication of having to carry $3,000 on the way back.

'All right.'

He pulled off the jacket that had been draped round Cal's shoulders. Then he produced a jack-knife from his pocket, opened it, spun the boy round and hacked through the knots. Cal's hands were swollen and blotched – and when the binding fell away Abe could see deep black and blue indentations around his wrists where the rope had bitten savagely into his flesh.

Standing in just his underwear Cal began to snivel as he massaged his wrists and the circulation began to flood back excruciatingly into his hands.

'See this?' said Abe, ignoring the boy's misery, and holding up the rope that he'd just unbound. 'I'm taking this with me, and if I find you've pulled just one more of your goddam tricks I'll use it to throttle you. Understand?'

'Yes, mister.'

'Then let's get going.'

He led the way up the first ladder with Cal following. Then with a final check to make sure the coast was clear outside, he clambered down the second ladder and waited for Cal to join him on the ground.

'Now just make straight for that hole,' whispered Abe. He seized tight hold of one of the boy's hands. 'Any noise and you know what I'm going to do.'

Cal led him slowly along the barn wall examining the ground carefully. There were one or two points where the timbers didn't meet flush with the ground, leaving apertures to the cement foundations. It was into one of these that he'd crawled the other night. He stopped, squatted down and peered under the timbers.

'This is it, mister. I've got to wriggle underneath to pull it out.'

Abe let go of his hand as the boy flattened himself against the sun-baked earth and eased his way under the barn. There was no way a man could have got in there. Cal all but disappeared leaving only his bare feet showing above ground. Abe was beginning to wonder whether this was another trick and the boy was intending to wriggle out of his reach. But after a few moments of scuffling Cal began to retreat, and at last emerged clutching a hessian sack.

He stood up and offered it to Abe.

'This is it mister. I told you the truth. Please will you let me go now?'

Abe took the sack and peered inside dubiously. It was stuffed with dollar bills. He nodded with satisfaction but made no reply to Cal's question. Instead, he wrapped his hand around the boy's mouth and led him struggling back to the ladder.

'Just get inside, boy, and no more trouble. I'll let you know when I've finished with you.'

They made their way up the ladder, into the barn, across the loft and down to where Seth and Chuck were waiting.

'You get it?' asked Seth eyeing the sack anxiously.

'Yup,' replied Abe matter-of-factly. 'Best count it to make sure he isn't double-crossing us.'

'I'm not, mister. I swear I never took anything.'

Seth emptied the contents of the sack on the table. 'You count it, Brother. I ain't much good at figuring.'

A quick check revealed that all the money was there.

'That's that, then,' said Abe with satisfaction. He piled the money back in the sack. 'Now for our next item of business.'

He fumbled in his belt and extracted the length of rope that had been used to tie Cal's hands. 'Just hold the boy a moment will you, Seth?'

'Sure thing,' grinned his brother, grabbing hold of Cal's shoulders.

Cal watched in horrified silence as Abe fashioned the rope into a noose and checked the suppleness of the knot.

'And now, boy,' he said with a leer, 'I'll just trouble you for the use of your neck.'

He slipped the noose over Cal's head and drew it tight.

Seth's eyes were glinting and he began to pant. 'Please, Abe, remember what they done to my hand.' He licked his lips expectantly. 'Let me do it, Brother. Please.'

TEN

'What in tarnation's going on in there?'

'Patience, son. Let them keep sweating.'

Jack Ellwood's voice was calm, but it did nothing to soothe Sefton's inner tension: he'd never enjoyed playing a waiting game over anything.

It was more than half an hour since that barn door had slammed shut and so far there had been neither sound nor movement down below them. Sefton had remained in position by the door caressing the Winchester against his cheek, waiting for just one opportunity to loose off a shot. What on earth were they doing in there, and what might they be doing to Cal?

The sun had steadily risen in the sky well above the ochre mountains in the distance, and the day was getting hot. Beads of sweat were coalescing on his brow and trickling down his temples. His joints were getting cramped from the continued inactivity, but he didn't dare shift his position in case he wasn't prepared for that one vital moment. He tried to put himself inside the minds of the men inside that barn. What could they be thinking? At the moment they couldn't be sure who had fired at them or how many they were dealing with. That was a factor in his favour. On the other hand – and his mind kept coming back to this reality with tiresome inevitability – they had the boy, and he knew – even if they didn't – that there was nothing he would do which might endanger the boy's life. He was chewing his lip in frustration when the barn door suddenly swung open.

At first all either of them could see was the darkness of the open doorway revealing nothing of the dimly lit interior behind. But then there was a movement and out stumbled Cal. For a wonderful second Hank thought that the boy had been released, but then he saw that there was a rope tied around the boy's neck in a noose. Immediately behind him came one of the Lancings holding the other end of the rope taut so that there was no possibility that Cal could put any distance between himself and his captor. In his other hand was a six-shooter with the muzzle nestling against the side of Cal's head.

Abe Lancing stepped out of the barn, keeping Cal between himself and the house. He looked up and addressed his unknown audience.

'Hey, you up there with the rifle. Don't try anything or the boy gets it. I mean it, mister.'

Hank muttered an oath. He was itching to pull that trigger and blast the trail-trash to kingdom come, but the risk to Cal was too great to be contemplated. Still, there was one thing he could do right away for the boy. First of all he edged the door open a little wider so that his voice would carry.

'Leave the kid alone mister,' he yelled. 'He ain't done you no harm. If you've got what you came for just take it and get out.'

Surely Cal would at least recognize his voice and know that he was close.

'That's just what we're about to do, mister,' Lancing yelled back. 'So don't you make no sudden move.'

He advanced a little, pushing Cal ahead with the muzzle of the gun. From the shadows behind him emerged his two companions. Hank derived some grim satisfaction from seeing that one of them had his hand wrapped in a bandanna. In his other hand he was carrying a sack which had not been visible when they arrived. No prizes for guessing what it contained.

'Hey, mister,' Lancing yelled again. 'You listening up there?'

'I'm listening.'

'We're about to move nice and easy towards our horses. Don't you go doing anything foolish you hear?'

'I hear.'

Lancing paused and looked around cautiously. Then he nodded to the others behind him and they made their way down to where the horses were tethered.

'Shucks,' muttered Ellwood, 'they're going to get clean away, and there ain't a goddammed thing we can do about it. Anyways, at least we were right about Chuck Morrison. That's him bringing up the rear. No-good rattlesnake.'

They watched helplessly as the tiny procession picked its way over to the horses and carefully mounted up. They kept Cal in the line of fire with the pistol pointed at his head all the time.

When they were mounted, with Cal up front astride Abe Lancing's saddle, Abe took off his hat and waved it in an ironic gesture of farewell.

'We're riding out nice and easy now. As long as you make no move we'll leave the boy ten minutes out on the trail. If you ride out after us before that he gets it.'

He reined in his horse to let the other two get ahead and then all three trotted off towards the bridge in single file.

If Sefton and Ellwood had found their vigil up in the farmhouse hard to endure, for Pat Ellwood, who had been posted in the tackle shed to guard the corral, it had been sheer torture. He, too, hated inactivity at any time, and to spend more than half an hour hardly daring to breathe had taxed his patience to the limit. The prospect of these three getting clean away, despite the efficiency of his pa's stakeout, was too much to bear.

As the trio approached the bridge he scuttled out of the shed with his Winchester in his hand and ran round behind the palings of the corral to try to level a shot.

From his vantage point at the window Jack Ellwood could see what his son was about to do and his blood ran cold. Surely Pat could realize that there was too much risk to the boy.

Thrusting open the window he tried to yell a warning.

'Pat, for Pete's sake don't try anything, boy! You hear me?'

The horses were just gathering pace in single file over the bridge when Abe Lancing, bringing up the rear, heard the shout and looked back in surprise. At the same moment, Pat Ellwood, unable to control his excitement, loosed off a shot aimed at bringing Lancing's horse down. His Winchester spat fire, but the buffet crumped into the pine balustrade of the bridge sending splinters of timber into the horse's face, The animal bucked in panic, and Lancing, who had been distracted just for a crucial moment by Ellwood's shout, found himself unbalanced. In an attempt to hold on to his seat he released his grip on Cal who now tipped out of his arm and rolled off the saddle almost under the horse's hooves. Before Lancing had a chance to react Cal had curled himself almost into a ball and spun himself over the side of the timbers to come to rest out of range under the bridge.

With a curse, Lancing dug his spurs into his horse's flanks and the three of them were away and on the trail, screened by some cottonwood trees before anyone had a chance to fire a second shot.

As the getaways' hooves clattered into the distance,

Hank Sefton came running out of the house down to the creek.

'Cal, Cal, boy – are you all right?'

He reached the bridge and called again, but there was no reply. Walking round to the side he crouched down and peered underneath. To his relief the boy was squatting under the timbers obviously alive.

'Cal, it's me – Uncle Hank. You can come out now.'

Slowly the slender figure in grubby woollen underwear squirmed its way out, stood upright, and flung itself into Sefton's arms.

'Boy, you sure look dirty. Even your hair's gone grey!'

He stepped back to get a better look at his nephew. The tumble off the horse didn't seem to have done Cal any harm, but his filthy condition and the livid weals on his wrists showed what sort of treatment he'd been getting. Sefton felt a swelling of rage as he added one more item to the account he was going to have to settle.

'Thanks for coming, Uncle Hank. I thought I was a real gonna.' Cal smiled shyly and grasped one of Hank's hands, as they walked slowly back to the house where Jack Ellwood was standing on the stoop.

Pat Ellwood came running up waving his Winchester in triumph.

'Hey, Pa, Mr Sefton. How was that for fancy shooting? I did it!'

'Best hold your tongue, boy,' growled Ellwood senior. 'That was one of the most dang foolish things I ever saw in my life.'

Pat looked crestfallen. 'But we got the boy, Pa.'

'No thanks to you, son. They could have blasted his head off, except that horse bucked.'

'Don't be too hard on him, Mr Ellwood,' said Hank. 'I guess Cal's grateful, anyway.'

'I sure am,' said Cal.

He turned and extended his hand towards Pat Ellwood who was skulking a couple of paces behind.

'Thanks.'

Pat Ellwood glanced at his father and grinned. 'My pleasure. Just feel free to call on me any time you want rescuing.'

Jack Ellwood shook his head in disgust. 'No thanks to you he didn't break his neck failing off that horse.'

'There wasn't any danger of that, Mr Ellwood,' said Cal cheerfully. 'My pa always said I was really good at falling off horses.'

Gus Donovan tried to keep his horse at a steady canter along the trail from Three Rocks, reluctant to lose time, and reluctant to tire the animal out. They'd divided their forces at the Double L ranch that morning. While Sefton, Jack Ellwood and Pat had ridden for the Riley homestead, Gus had been dispatched to Three Rocks for the sheriff. He hadn't been happy about the arrangement, suspecting he was being cut out of the action, but he couldn't really contend Jack Ellwood's point that he'd swallowed too much smoke in the bunkhouse to be fit for a real shoot-out if it came to that. He'd arrived at Three Rocks just after sun-up and had had the satisfaction of tumbling Matt Westlake out of bed. It had taken some time to persuade Westlake to take the same view of last night's activities as they had, but he'd finally agreed to round up a few riders and head on out to the Riley spread.

With his task accomplished, Gus had seen no particular reason to hang about in Three Rocks waiting for Westlake to get a posse together when things might be warming up elsewhere. So he had ridden on ahead in case he was needed.

He had met nobody on the journey so far until he reached the point where the track started to descend

towards Salto Creek. From here there was a good view of
the trail as it unwound from the cottonwoods and willows
that marked the watercourse below, and it was from here
that Donovan caught sight of three riders coming up fast
from the direction of the Riley spread. He reined in his
horse under the shelter of an overhanging cliff and
shaded his eyes against the morning sunlight.

It was a quiet trail at any time, but it was the speed of
the riders which really caught his attention. Law-abiding
folk never hurried in these parts. Donovan strained his
eyes to see if he could make out any distinguishing char-
acteristics as the riders approached. Two of the men were
completely unfamiliar to him, but the third was wearing a
jacket he recognized. Surely this was Chuck Morrison?
When he was satisfied that his identification was correct,
Gus backed his horse up to a little copse of cedar trees that
stood just to one side of the trail. He dismounted, tethered his horse behind a tree and slid his Winchester out of
its saddle-scabbard. Then he positioned himself behind a
fallen tree trunk so as to have a clear view of about a
hundred yards of the trail ahead of him.

He'd woken up that morning feeling as though he had
a pound of soot lodged in his guts, but now the surge of
excitement at the prospect of real action drove all the
physical effects of last night's drama completely out of his
mind. It was three against one and he was taking a terrible
risk. But his self-confidence was bolstered by the fact that
he was going to have the advantage of surprise as the
riders turned the corner towards him, plus the security of
knowing that Westlake and his men wouldn't be far
behind him. There was also the possibility that Sefton and
the Ellwoods were following hard on the men's heels from
the other direction, unless, of course. . . . But no, he
preferred not to think about what might have happened at
the homestead, He settled himself with the carbine

nestling comfortably on the tree trunk as the trampling of hooves grew louder.

He waited until all three men were clearly in sight about fifty yards ahead of him and then the Winchester barked, kicking sharply into his shoulder as he whanged a shell into the track a few yards in front of the leading horse. There was a crack and a ferocious spurt of dust as the bullet cleaved a small rock in two and sent shards of flint flying in all directions. As he'd anticipated, this demonstration of fire power brought all three riders to a skidding stop. The next shot was aimed over their heads and crumped into the overhang behind them, dislodging trickles of shale and grit on to their hats.

Donovan stood up cautiously and levelled the Winchester straight at the chest of the leading rider.

'Hold it right there and get your hands above your heads where I can see them.'

'What is this, mister?' demanded Abe Lancing in genuine puzzlement. 'A goddam hold up?'

'It's no highwayman,' said Morrison, his lip curling in disgust. 'It's the sidewinder who stole my job at the Double L ranch.'

'Off your horses, trash, and keep your hands up.'

Donovan moved a little closer as none of the men made any attempt to dismount.

'You hear what I said? Get down off them horses real slow and keep your hands high.'

'Kind of ambitious, aren't you, mister?' sneered Abe. 'First you steal my friend's job, now you want to take on all three of us.'

He still showed no sign of obeying Donovan's command, and the other two were obviously intent on following his lead. Donovan decided to back up his authority with hot lead. He raised the Winchester, and without any further attempt at parley he fired a shot that zapped past Lancing's ear to whang into the rocks over his head.

Lancing's horse had already been half spooked by Pat Ellwood's shot back on the bridge, and now the detonation of the cartridge and the crack as the rock behind its head splintered, unnerved it again. But this time, instead of rearing, it started forward, free of any restraint from Lancing who still had his hands in the air.

Before Donovan had time to collect his wits, the horse had sprung towards him striking Gus a glancing blow and knocking him to one side as the Winchester clattered uselessly to the ground. The next moment he was staring into the pistols that Morrison and the other Lancing had slicked immediately out of their holsters, while behind him Abe Lancing was recovering control of his horse and wheeling it around.

'Guess you was a little *too* ambitious this time, Gus,' smirked Morrison as he levelled the Colt at Donovan's head. 'Now get your hands real high.'

Donovan had no alternative but to comply. The Winchester had fallen beyond reach and there seemed to be six-shooters trained on him from all directions. Morrison slipped off his horse, walked over, and unbuckled Donovan's gunbelt.

Seth Lancing fanned back the hammer on his Colt.

'Which one of us is going to get the pleasure of this pilgrim?'

Morrison held up his hand. 'My pleasure, I think. I'm the one with the grievance. And anyway a bullet'd be too quick.'

'Come on, man,' said Abe impatiently. 'We've no time to lose.'

Disregarding Abe's impatience Morrison backed Donovan off the trail against one of the cedars.

'Hey, Seth,' he called over his shoulder. 'Job for you.

Bring your rope over here and tie his hands real tight.'

Seth glanced at his brother, shrugged, dismounted and hurried across with a length of rope. When Donovan's hands had been secured in front of him, Morrison returned to his horse and unloosed his stockwhip from the saddle. Then he came and stood in front of Donovan.

'Let's call this one tit for tat, Gus,' he said grimly. 'I'm gonna repay a licking with a licking. I warned you to watch your back.'

They passed the end of the rope over a convenient tree branch and stretched Donovan so that the toes of his boots were scarcely touching the ground. Morrison uncoiled the whip and gave it a preliminary shake.

'Guess we're almost ready then. See to his shirt, Seth.'

Seth Lancing walked across eagerly and tore Donovan's shirt apart, from the collar down. He faced Donovan with a leer, allowing his hand to trace an exploratory path over Donovan's bare chest.

'Mighty purdy body you got there, mister. Real shame it's going to get all cut up.'

'Get your filthy paw off me, trash,' said Donovan. He spat, accurately, in Lancing's face.

Lancing wiped his face and turned to Morrison. 'Save a bit of him for me, Chuck. Please. I just gotta give him a few.'

'Sure,' grinned Morrison. 'There's enough meat on that carcass for everyone.'

He stood back, measuring the length of the whip on the ground, and then scientifically got down to business.

Donovan had steeled himself for the pain and was determined not to give his tormentors the satisfaction of hearing him yell, but Morrison almost succeeded in breaking his resolution with the first lash. The whip sliced through the air to land just below Donovan's shoulders, the tip curling under his arm and flicking like fire round into his chest.

The impact and the shattering pain nearly caused him to lose his precarious footing and dangle suspended only by his wrists, but he managed to dig his toes into the ground. He began to shiver uncontrollably as behind him Morrison gathered himself and applied the second stroke, landing it just a little below the previous one and once again sending the tip scorching round into his belly.

The blood began to sing in his ears as Morrison established a steady rhythm, pausing between the lashes and aiming each one so as to raise a criss-crossed pattern of welts from Donovan's neck to his belt, Seth was yelling encouragement with every stroke, but Morrison needed no inspiration to settle his personal score.

Despite the obvious pleasure his brother was deriving from this spectacle, Abe Lancing was getting anxious. He glanced nervously back at the trail they'd just covered, half expecting to see a cloud of white dust heralding the imminent arrival of their pursuers, but all seemed quiet. Then he turned his head in the other direction and saw what he'd feared: not just a dust cloud but a group of riders coming fast from the direction of Three Rocks. It was time for the party to stop.

'Looks like we're going to get company,' he yelled, making for his horse. 'Come on, will you. We've got to get off the trail!'

Morrison looked over his shoulder, coiled up the whip reluctantly, and sprang into his saddle. Seth, almost unwilling to believe that he could have been cheated out of his turn with the whip, took a moment longer to come to terms with reality. Then he landed a vicious valedictory kick at Donovan's legs and followed the others at a gallop out of sight through the trees. . . .

'Aren't you going after them, Uncle Hank?'

'You bet I am, boy. But we need to do it properly.

Sheriff's been alerted to raise a decent posse to track them down.'

They had walked on back to the farmhouse and rummaged about for some spare clothes for Cal to put on. Hank Sefton had tried to keep his voice as calm as possible, but he was itching for action. At least, now, he'd seen the faces of his sister's killers – and they would be imprinted in his memory until he'd seen them brought to justice.

'Sure was a pity they got away with all that money,' said Cal, pulling on a fresh set of dungarees.

'Sure was a pity you didn't bother to tell us about it in the first place,' said Hank, curtly. 'You would have saved us all a lot of trouble.'

Cal looked crestfallen. 'Yessir,' he mumbled. Then he added, 'I really am sorry, Uncle Hank, but I did it for Pa. And then when I found out he was dead I didn't know whether to tell you about it or not. And then it was too late.'

'No use crying over spilt milk,' said Ellwood. 'We've got the boy back and that was the most important thing. The money belongs to the bank anyway. And now, if you've made that boy respectable, perhaps we can get back to the ranch.'

Sefton shook his head. 'You, Pat and Cal, yes. But I'm heading towards Three Rocks. Sheriff ought to be due out if Gus has done his job, and this time I'm not letting the trail go cold.'

Ellwood inclined his head. 'All right son, but be careful. Those varmints have got nothing to lose – so don't give them a chance to fire the first shot.'

Cal gave Sefton an almost proprietorial stare and then held out his hand.

'Good luck, Uncle Hank.'

Sefton glanced down at the scarred wrist, set his jaw,

and shook hands without a word. They split up accordingly, and Sefton put Rayo into a sharp canter along the trail to Three Rocks. Here at least there was no difficulty in following the tracks left by three galloping horses. He was just wondering where the fugitives would choose to strike across country when a few hundred yards ahead of him he spotted a cluster of horses drawn up by the side of the trail. He checked Rayo and approached cautiously. Closer up he recognized Westlake and a group of riders crouched or kneeling on the ground examining something. Sefton dismounted and joined the group.

Gus Donovan was lying stripped to the waist face down on the ground, his back a raw lattice of welts.

'What in. . . ?' exclaimed Sefton.

Westlake looked up. 'We just cut him down. Apparently Chuck Morrison's had his revenge.'

ELEVEN

Reining in his horse, Chuck Morrison held up his hand.

'Guess we're gonna have to take it a bit easier. These animals are getting all lathered up. No sense in running the legs off them.'

They'd pressed the horses hard for the best part of half an hour as the sun rose steadily in the sky. Besides, the terrain was much more broken now – troughs and ridges of dry sun-baked earth scattered with sage brush, the occasional saguaro, and countless treacherous small rocks. Easy country for a fast moving horse to trespass into a gopher hole, break its leg and throw its rider. They couldn't afford any accident.

Seth Lancing, covertly checking down at his unhealed thigh, showed no disposition to challenge Morrison's order. The speed and roughness of the ride had played tarnation with the wound, while his mutilated hand was throbbing painfully. For the moment, anyway, they were in Morrison's hands. They had agreed to make for the cabin where they'd overnighted the day before, and then to split up. Only Morrison knew the route so they had to let him lead. The arrangement suited Morrison, too. As long as they were in strange territory they needed him.

They set their horses into an easy lope as he led them

down a defile towards a rill. On the other side a narrow track led up a sandstone escarpment towards a ridge which would offer them a clear retrospective view of the country they had just crossed. They would easily be able to see if they were being followed. They had been travelling in a wide arc and the cabin was only a mile or so beyond the undulating terrain that lay over the ridge, but Morrison kept the geography of the situation to himself. The less they knew for the moment, the better.

'Sure is tarnation hot down here,' muttered Seth as they picked their way down to the watercourse. 'This what it's like all the way along?'

'Yup.'

'You think they'll follow us this far?'

'Depends who it is,' said Morrison laconically. 'If it was just a bunch of cowboys out for a ride, they'll probably give up. It isn't easy to follow a trail through water. But if it was a posse then they'll stick to us.'

'Kind of looked like a posse to me,' said Abe. 'I should know – I've seen a few in my time.'

They followed the stream carefully until Morrison signalled them to break away and make towards the ridge on the far side. Once they had reached the crest they dismounted. Tethering their horses on the reverse slope they positioned themselves in the shade of a rock and surveyed the route they had just traversed. As Morrison had anticipated, they were able to look back on the best part of an hour's ride. As far as they could see, there was nobody behind them so far.

'Guess it won't hurt us to rest a while,' he said. 'As long as we keep our eyes open.'

The sun was almost directly overhead and the temptation to dawdle the afternoon away was all but overwhelming. With scarcely any sleep the night before, a ride before dawn, the tension of that hour in the barn, and the excite-

ment of their escape they were all at the limit of their
strength.

And, of course, Morrison in particular needed to think.
The Lancings had cut him in on their predicament
because they had needed him to kidnap the boy, but with
the money safely stowed now in Abe's saddle-pouches, and
familiar country not far away, his value to them was about
to drop away to zilch. Not that Morrison was anxious to
prolong their acquaintance for a moment longer than
necessary. Their hides were on the line for robbery and
murder, whereas he was only an accessory – albeit also with
a hand in an abortive kidnap. The sooner he was out of
their company the better.

Covertly he studied their faces as they scanned the
distant horizon. As far as he knew, he'd given them no
opportunity to talk to each other privately, but he'd be
readier to trust a rattlesnake than take a chance on his life
with either of these two. Fortunately it looked as though
he was really dealing with one and a half. It was clear
enough that Seth was suffering badly. Fresh blood was
seeping through Seth's pants and, of course, his left hand
was now as useless as his brain.

They drank copiously from their canteens and rested
up for half an hour. Still nobody appeared on the trail
behind them. But that was as much as Morrison was willing to risk. He agreed with Abe: only posses rode with the
sort of determination that he'd seen back there on the
trail. Obviously, they'd have to stop to take care of
Donovan and find out what he could tell them, but then
they would push on. He wondered what sort of price had
been put on the Lancings' heads. There was nothing like
the prospect of reward money for keeping a pursuit
hot. . . .

'You sure you want to stick this out?'

Matt Westlake's tone was decidedly sceptical as he half turned in his saddle to address Hank Sefton. He had made no secret of his dislike of amateurs messing in the work of the law. Especially amateurs with a personal grudge against their quarry. It made for poor judgement at critical moments.

'Kind of an unnecessary question, isn't it, Sheriff?'

Sefton pulled his hat a little more firmly over his eyes and jutted his chin.

'Maybe I should be asking you the same question. After all, you were the one who called a halt last time.'

'True enough. And I was right. But this time we've got all the men we need. I'm not about to let go. And now we've got a real tracker.'

He nodded ahead towards a half-caste who was leading the group on a sorrel pony, his eyes never lifting from the ground in front of him, Indian Joe was Westlake's most reliable bloodhound.

They had seen Gus Donovan escorted back to the Double L by a member of the posse and had resumed the pursuit at a controlled pace, despite Sefton's appeals for speed. Westlake had made it clear that he intended to play this pursuit long, knowing that he might have to conserve the horses' strength for an unpredictable ride across wild country. So he restricted the pace to a steady canter where the state of the ground permitted, and slowed right down wherever the trail became uncertain.

As Sefton made no further comment Westlake pointed towards the low hills and ridges that were rising ahead of them.

'If they've taken that route I wouldn't be surprised if we're under observation right now.'

Sefton shaded his eyes and peered ahead, but there was no hope of picking out individual figures against the sandstone. If they were going to be bushwhacked the first they'd know about it would be the crack of a rifle from somewhere above them. He wondered momentarily whether his privileged position near the head of the posse was such a good idea. . . .

Morrison had still not arranged his thoughts properly by the time they reached the cabin in mid afternoon. The Lancings had gone strangely silent too, with none of their habitual brotherly banter. They all dismounted to dip their hats in the stream, pouring the water over their sweat-streaked heads. When they had refilled their canteens, Morrison secured his own canteen to his saddle and hefted down his stock whip. It was still flecked with blood and scraps of skin from its recent encounter with Donovan's back. He examined it with distaste and then crouched down, uncoiled the whip, plunged it in the stream and drew the entire length of the lash between the thumb and forefinger of his gloved hand.

'Well, I guess this is the parting of the ways, *compadres*,' he said, looking across at the Lancings who were sprawled in an apparent state of exhaustion on a couple of rocks nearby. 'You know your way out of here towards Sedona Springs and the Santa Fe track. So let's have my thousand and I'll be quitting.'

The two brothers exchanged glances and then Abe replied, 'Sure thing. Seth, why don't you count out Chuck his money?'

Seth got painfully to his feet, approached his brother's horse and unbuckled the flap of one of the saddle-pouches. He pulled out a fistful of greenbacks and then turned to his brother who was standing a little way behind him. As if the thought had only just struck him he said, 'Sure don't know why you gave me this job, Brother. You know I never was much good at any kind of figuring work.'

Abe chuckled.

'Guess that's right. But now I come to think of it, I don't much care for the arithmetic of the situation anyway. Three into three thousand ain't as much as two into three thousand.'

As he spoke, his right hand moved to his holster, but Morrison was ready for him. Without wasting a second on trying to rise from his crouching position beside the stream he flicked up the whip accurately, curling it around Seth's neck and dragging him helplessly back towards him. It was an unfair contest of strength, as Morrison had anticipated, because Seth had been limping from the pain of his reopened wound and had a disabled hand to contend with as well. With a strangled cry of rage, fumbling impotently with his one sound hand at the lash which had locked around his neck, he tumbled headlong in front of Morrison obscuring his brother's line of fire. The revolver hung uselessly in Abe Lancing's hand as Morrison released the whip, grabbed Seth by the scruff of the neck and applied the muzzle of his Colt to Seth's temple.

'Don't neither of you move,' said Morrison curtly, 'or I'll blow his brains out.'

'He means it, Abe,' gasped Seth, as Morrison's grip tightened on his collar and he found himself being lifted to his feet. 'For Pete's sake don't move.'

'As I was saying,' continued Morrison as if nothing unusual had happened, 'it's time for the parting of the ways. Sorry it couldn't have been a bit more amicable. I'd be mighty obliged, Abe, if you'd kindly holster your gun and then kick your gunbelt over to me.'

Abe Lancing hesitated. 'Supposing I don't, mister? What then?'

Morrison made no reply, but fanned back the hammer on his Colt. Seth screamed as he heard the click.

'Please, Abe. You know what he'll do. Just put your gun away!'

But Abe Lancing still made no move.

'Seems to me, mister,' he said, almost as if he couldn't see his brother sweating and squirming in Morrison's remorseless grip, 'that my arithmetic still holds up. Two into three thousand is a nice little figure. Guess it doesn't really matter who the two are as long as I'm one of them.'

'Are you offering me a deal over your brother's head, you rattlesnake?'

'I'm just saying that two's company while three ain't any. So what if I don't put my gun away? Maybe I should just leave you to even up the arithmetic yourself.'

Seth began to sob in fear and frustration. 'Abe, you no-good rattlesnake, I'm your brother. Don't let him kill me, please. We're in this together, goddammit.'

There was a terrible silence while both Seth and Morrison waited for Abe Lancing to make his move. He took his time over it while his brother writhed at Morrison's feet.

'Why, Seth,' he smirked ironically, as he surveyed a darkening stain on the front of this brother's corduroys, 'I do believe you've pissed your pants. Bet you ain't done that since you was a kid.'

Finally Abe made up his mind. He dropped his hand slowly and holstered his gun. Then he unhitched his gunbelt, let it drop to the ground, and kicked it over towards Morrison.

Putting his own Colt away, Morrison relieved Seth of his sidearms and threw him to the ground in a quivering heap. He collected Abe's gunbelt and slung it over his shoulder. Then he trained his gun once again on Abe Lancing.

'Back to the arithmetic, mister. Let's see you count out the money nice and easy.'

Abe gathered the bills which had fallen to the ground when Seth had received the whip around his neck, and methodically counted out $1,000. He made as if to walk over and offer them to Morrison.

'Something wrong with your arithmetic, pardner,' said Morrison, holding up his hand to halt Lancing in mid step. 'I agree with your calculation. Two into three thousand is a mighty fair sum. So just count me out another five hundred and you can argue with your brother about how you divide up the rest.'

'Abe,' snarled his brother from the ground, 'you gonna let him get away with this?'

'Seems like I ain't got much choice,' said Abe eyeing the Colt which was still levelled at his belly. He turned and raked another fistful of dollars out of the saddle pouch. When Abe had counted it out again, Morrison gestured with the muzzle of his revolver.

'Just stow it nice and easy in my saddle-bag, please.'

When everything had been arranged to his satisfaction, Morrison mounted up and directed the Lancings into the cabin. Then he fired a couple of shots into the air to spook their horses into a terrified gallop and made off in a cloud of dust and scattered tumbleweed.

The Lancings rushed out of the cabin fearing that their horses might have already disappeared. But the dangling strap of the open saddle-pouch on Abe's horse had ensnared itself in a gorse bush as the animal brushed past, bringing the horse to a squirming stop.

Abe rushed over and extracted his Winchester from its scabbard. Spinning round, he dropped to one knee, took careful aim and discharged a shell towards Morrison's retreating back just before he could disappear from sight.

TWELVE

Matt Westlake coiled up the whip and handed it to Hank Sefton.

'Reckon you might as well take this back to Donovan when this is over. He might appreciate it as a souvenir.'

Sefton took the whip and roped it behind his saddle. The gravel at the edge of the rill was scuffled and marked. Obviously there had been some sort of disturbance here, but what, exactly, and how long ago?

Indian Joe had dismounted and was carefully examining the ground all around the cabin. Finally he faced Westlake and spread out his hands.

'Uh, uh,' muttered Westlake. 'They separated. I knew it.'

Sefton scratched his head in irritation. A decision was going to have to be made here, but he wanted to postpone it as long as possible. He glanced beyond Westlake at the tracks leading away from the cabin. One horse only – so presumably Morrison. He walked his horse alongside the traces of hoofprints to the point where they turned and left the cabin out of sight. Then he trotted back to where Westlake and Joe were talking under their voices.

'Whoever was riding this horse weren't too comfortable. He'd been shot.'

Sefton indicated the tracks he'd just examined.

'Good sleuthing, son. Joe just told me the same thing. Prints are uneven.'

'I didn't notice the hoofprints,' said Sefton. 'I was concentrating on the bloodstains just around the bend.'

'What?'

'Come and see for yourself.'

He led the sheriff to where just visible on a white rock that projected from the dust there was a faint but unmistakable splash of fresh blood.

'Mind if I ride on a little ways? I may spot something else.'

Westlake nodded. The other riders needed a rest, anyway. Sefton trotted on for a half-mile or so. The path led downwards through scattered conifers and then straightened out into more open scrub country. A little way beyond, Sefton caught sight of a saddled horse trying to crop the sparse vegetation. He approached warily, his carbine drawn at the ready. Near where the horse was standing the sand was scuffled where the rider had obviously taken a tumble. There were further splashes of blood to be seen scattered around. Beyond this there were clear signs in the dirt that someone had been crawling away.

Sefton picked his way carefully through the sage brush, pausing every few moments to listen. At last, as he approached a depression in the ground he thought he heard a groan of pain. There in front of him stretched out face up in a pool of his own blood was Chuck Morrison.

He was still alive. As Sefton knelt beside him and lifted his head Morrison opened his eyes and stared vacantly at him.

'Shot me, mister,' he murmured. 'Splintered my backbone. Don't try and move me.'

It was obvious his time was running out fast. Already swarms of black ants had gathered on the blood-soaked sand around his body. His lips were moving with exaggerated deliberation as he tried to frame some more words.

'Mister, I can't make it. Finish me off. Please.'

Sefton considered this request for a moment. Then he stood up and levelled his rifle. He would have no compunction about pulling the trigger, but as Morrison stared up at him with glazed eyes he paused to reflect. It was true that he had no personal grudge against Morrison as he did against the Lancings. Morrison was not implicated in the deaths of Wilma and Jess. But he was guilty by association, and he'd certainly played a key part in the kidnapping of Cal, Sefton thought bitterly of the boy's wrists, and the scars around them he was probably going to carry for the rest of his life. Even if Morrison hadn't tied the knots he'd gone along with it and let the boy suffer. Then there was the question of what he'd done to Gus Donovan. It was a fair guess that if Westlake had not turned up Gus might actually have been flogged to death.

'Come on, mister,' croaked Morrison again. 'What are you waiting for? Finish me off.'

Slowly Sefton lowered his rifle.

'Can't oblige you, Morrison,' he replied, his lip curling in contempt. 'I don't reckon you're even worth a shell. So you can lie there and feed the ants with your worthless carcass.'

Ignoring the rasping pleas for deliverance he turned on his heel and walked back and gathered Morrison's horse. Then he trotted Rayo back to the others.

'Find anything?' asked Westlake.

'Morrison. He's finished.'

Westlake pursed his lips. 'I don't think we'll waste time on a burial party.'

'No need. The ants'll do the job. Them and the buzzards.'

'Anything in the saddle-bags?'

'Nope,' said Sefton. 'Seems he went to an awful lot of trouble for nothing.'

Abe Lancing glanced impatiently over his shoulder, His horse was barely travelling at a jogtrot, but Seth seemed to have increasing difficulty in keeping up. The relentless sun was now clearly pitched over into the western sky, and he reckoned they were about five miles from Sedona Springs. There was no way they could push the horses, though. It had been a ferocious day's ride made longer by the necessity of occasional backtracking to confuse any pursuit. His own mount was lathered and breathing unevenly, and he guessed Seth's was in the same state – as far as he could make out across the fifty yards or so that Seth had allowed to open up between them.

But it was Seth himself who was giving most cause for concern. The last time they had stopped to rest the horses after leaving the cabin, Abe had been alarmed by his brother's appearance. The leg wound had obviously reopened, and his mutilated hand hung useless by his side. His other hand kept rubbing ineffectually at the weal left round his neck by the lash of Morrison's whip. His face, despite the burning heat of the sun, was the colour of dirty putty. Abe wondered whether he had made the right choice back there at the cabin. He hadn't just been teasing his brother when he offered his alternative way of dividing up the spoils. He was clear enough in his mind that Morrison would make a better and more reliable companion on the trail than his wounded useless brother. Seth was a liability – probably had been since he stopped that bullet back in Halesville – but in the end blood ties had proved too strong for Abe's instinct. He had had plenty of time to rethink and regret his generosity in the last couple of hours, however. And once again his mind was dwelling on the arithmetic of their situation. With

Morrison lying on his back in the dirt and his self apportioned share of the money back in Abe's saddle-pouch, Abe was wondering why the money had to be divided at all. Once the thought of the three thousand all to himself had crept into his mind, he was having difficulty shifting it. And, as Seth drifted further back behind him on the trail, so he was drifting further out of the picture in Abe's thoughts.

He looked back again. Seth was hunched over his saddle seemingly holding his position only by gripping the saddle horn with his good hand. The horse was walking mechanically with no assistance or encouragement from its rider. Seth was clearly running out of the will or strength to continue.

Abe reined in his horse and waited for Seth to catch up. As he approached, Abe saw that his eyes were closed and that a trail of blood from his leg wound led all the way down from his thigh to his stirrup shoe.

He said nothing for a moment as Seth's horse came alongside and stopped. Seth's eyes opened blearily as he became suddenly aware of the cessation of motion. He gazed at Abe and then slid wearily, helplessly, from the saddle.

'Guess I'm about all in,' he croaked, as he crawled to a nearby boulder and propped himself up against it.

'Reckon you are, Brother,' said Abe, noting that Seth didn't even have the strength to walk to the rock.

'Gimme a drink, Abe. Please.'

Abe dismounted and unlaced his canteen. They had refilled both canteens at the cabin, and taken Morrison's as well, but there wasn't much left in any of them – with no prospect of a refill till Sedona Springs. He walked across, unstoppered the canteen, and offered it to his brother. Seth drank greedily, draining the canteen to the last drop.

Abe stood watching his suffering with folded arms and

an air of total detachment. His own thirst was a torment, but he was unwilling to surrender to it in front of his brother. Suddenly, despite the heat, Seth started to shiver uncontrollably. Through rattling teeth he looked up at Abe and spoke.

'Can't see myself climbing back on that horse, Brother. Guess we'd best try and find a spot to bivouac out here for the night.'

Abe contemplated the pathetic figure in front of him in silence.

'What about it, Abe?'

There was a sudden note of querulous anxiety in Seth's voice at his brother's uncharacteristic unwillingness to take charge of the situation.

Abe hesitated for a few seconds longer and then made up his mind.

'Guess you're right about not being able to make it back up on your horse. . . .'

Seth Lancing relaxed visibly against the boulder. Evidently he had been afraid that his brother would force him to continue the ride.

'. . . so I figure from here on I'll be riding alone,' he continued imperturbably.

It took a few seconds for Seth to take in the import of what Abe had just said. Then, despite his pain, he tried to struggle to his feet.

'Whaddya mean, ride alone? We're *compadres*, ain't we? Half that money's mine as well.'

'I'm just facing facts, Brother. You aren't gonna make it.'

'I know I'm not going to make it today, but I will tomorrow after we've rested up. I'll be all right.'

The effort of trying to stand was too much for him, and Seth slithered helplessly back to the ground.

'See what I mean?' said Abe. 'You aren't going to make

it, Brother, not today, not tomorrow, not any time.'

Seth looked up with real fear in his eyes as he came to terms with the horror of what his brother was about to do.

'Abe, you ain't gonna leave me out here as coyote meat? Please. I swear I'll be all right tomorrow. I'll ride with you, Abe, just like it's always been.'

Abe Lancing shook his head and sighed. 'I know it's kind of hard, Seth, but there's no point in me going down along with you. You need a doctor bad, and I just don't see any around here, do you?'

Seth Lancing began to snivel.

'No, but there's a doc in Sedona Springs and we aren't that far. Please, Abe. Take me with you.'

'Sorry, boy. I think your luck's finally run out. Best make yourself comfortable here. I'll leave you the food and your Colts.'

'What about my share of the money?' screamed Seth, panicking impotently. 'You gonna leave me that, too?'

'Don't see no need,' said Abe. 'Ain't much you can spend it on round here.'

Seth's eyes began to roll desperately as he cast round for something to persuade his brother not to abandon him.

'Abe, please. I tell you what, Abe, you can have my share of the money. Just take it, Abe. I don't want it. But don't leave me out here.'

'That's mighty generous of you, Brother, but I guess I've already got your share of the money and like I said, I don't need your company any more.'

Abe bent down, removed his brother's sidearms from their holsters and emptied their chambers into the sand. He didn't want a bullet in his back as he rode off. He tossed the remaining provisions down beside his brother and remounted.

'So long, Seth. It's been nice knowing you.'

Abe Lancing put his weary horse into a jogtrot as Seth's pathetic screams, pleas and curses followed him across the dust.

'Guess we all know where we'll be bedding down for the night.'

Matt Westlake turned in his saddle and grinned at the rest of the posse.

'Hey boys, how you all fancy a night in Sedona Springs?'

There was a mirthful cheer at this suggestion. Sedona Springs was better supplied with entertainment than Three Rocks – especially of the feminine kind. Once they had restarted the pursuit from the cabin there wasn't much doubt about the way the hoofprints were headed. There was only one logical place and it didn't take an expert tracker to work it out.

Hank Sefton jogged along comfortably beside Westlake, scarcely bothering to keep his eyes fixed on the dirt in front of them in case the tracks deviated. The sun was well down in the sky now, but although their horses were tired they still had enough spirit to maintain a steady trot.

Which was more than their quarry were capable of, reflected Sefton as, from time to time, he stared down at their tracks. Only a walking pace, apparently, and one of the horses was being ridden very unevenly. He thought back on what Cal had told him of his experiences with the Lancings. Seth was twice wounded now and he must have had a hell of a day in the saddle. A grim smile of satisfaction crossed Sefton's sweat-stained features. It would be a shame if the end came too quickly.

Sefton's pleasant thoughts were interrupted as Indian Joe who, as usual, was a few paces ahead, held up his hand and brought them to a halt. The trail immediately in front of them was scuffed, and from there onwards only one set of hoofprints proceeded towards Sedona Springs.

Matt Westlake shielded his eyes and looked around in all directions.

'Now, where in tarnation?'

It was clear enough that one horse and rider hadn't made it further than here, but where were they? The country they were riding through was mostly scrub and open except for occasional gullies and boulder-strewn ridges on one side of the trail. They dismounted to take a closer look at the prints in the sand.

'Best keep your Colt drawn, Sefton,' advised Westlake. 'A wounded rattlesnake's more dangerous than a healthy one – and that's what we've got here.'

They followed the scuff marks in the sand to a nearby boulder where Sefton pointed silently to traces of blood on the ground.

'Guess he ain't far off,' muttered Westlake. 'Come out, come out, wherever you are,' he cooed softly as they began to explore further on.

They soon found the horse. It had wandered round into a gully in search of something to eat. Sefton examined it carefully.

'Been ridden right off its feet, so I guess the other one must be in the same state.'

'In that case the other polecat'll be lucky if he makes it to Sedona Springs.'

Matt Westlake contemplated the horse for a moment.

'Well, let's find our wounded rattlesnake. No use leaving him here for some other sucker to trip over.'

From here on the terrain was mostly rocks and boulders and there were no easy bootprints to follow. A quarter of a mile ahead the furrows lodged up against the foot of a sandstone mesa offering a fugitive all sorts of possibilities for shelter. They divided their forces and started combing in a broad sweep towards the cliff.

Sefton's heart suddenly thumped as he came across a

trace of fresh blood on the shingle by his boot. He looked around. All the other members of the posse some distance away had their eyes fixed on the ground ahead of them. He was about to call them over when he was suddenly seized by the urge to finish this one alone. Now he had the occasional bloodstains to help him in the right direction and they were leading him around a turn in the cliff face. He could see that what from a distance had appeared to be a simple crevice in the face of the rock was actually the entrance to a narrow downward leading gully. He strained his eyes in all directions but the rock walls on either side screened off the sunlight, leaving nothing but shadows.

Then, momentarily, in the gloom ahead of him came the faint but unmistakeable rattling of disturbed rocks. The hairs on the back of Sefton's neck started to rise as he remembered Sheriff Westlake's words about wounded rattlesnakes. Seth Lancing would certainly have his sidearms and might even have a rifle. There had been none in the scabbard on the abandoned horse. Hank proceeded cautiously, trying to make no sound as he advanced, almost crouching, down the gully. A few moments later he again heard a sound as if of boots scrunching on gravel. The narrowness of the gully and the rock faces towering on either side tended to distort every sound, so it was difficult to pinpoint direction and distance. There was no doubting the reality of what happened next, however.

There was a muffled detonation and a flick of flame as, ahead of him, Lancing, invisible behind cover, aimed a shot with his Colt. Sefton heard the bullet whine past his head and crack into the rock face behind him. But before he could duck, a second shot clipped the flesh of his upper left arm and then pinged harmlessly away into the scree.

Sefton yelped – more in anger than in pain – flattened

himself and clutched, cursing, at his arm. Blood was
already seeping through his shirt sleeve. He wondered
briefly whether this enterprise on his own had been such
a good idea. But there was no time for self-reproach as up
ahead on a ledge he saw a movement. Seth Lancing,
perhaps fancying that his second shot had done lethal
damage, had edged himself outwards to get a better view
of his intended victim.

Still lying flat among dry grass and loose boulders,
Sefton manoeuvred his right arm straight out, so that his
Colt was ready to aim as soon as he could get a clear
enough target. For the moment he scarcely dared to lift
his head in case Lancing had his revolver ready levelled.

There was another movement ahead as Lancing
squirmed for position. Sefton seized his opportunity and
his Colt barked out a bullet that crumped harmlessly into
the sandstone above Lancing's head.

But now Lancing had a target to aim at. He raised
himself slightly, sighted and fired. This time his shot struck
a rock inches from Sefton's head sending splinters and
shards of flint into his face. He was so convinced by the
pain that he must have been hit, that he blindly emptied
the chamber of his six-shooter in a series of desperate
shots towards where he figured Lancing had fired from.

His aim was wild, but the volley of bullets caused
Lancing to attempt to roll his way out of trouble. As he did
so, the side of the ledge on which he was perched gave way
beneath him and he tumbled helplessly in a shower of
earth and shingle to the foot of the gully almost at a
surprised Sefton's feet.

Sefton was on his feet immediately with his other Colt
drawn ready for action. But, as he rushed forward, he realized that the danger was past.

Lancing was sprawled out on his back with his one good
hand empty – having lost his six-shooter in the tumble. He

made no attempt to rise as Sefton stood over him.

'Don't shoot, mister. I ain't armed any more.'

Sefton stood and contemplated the pathetic figure in front of him for a moment. What trash! Lancing's pants were bloodstained and his left hand was wrapped in a bandanna that was also stiff with congealed blood. His face was cut and bruised. He was clearly finished, yet, amazingly he still seemed to think he had the right to live.

'Please, mister,' he begged, 'get me out of this. I need help bad.'

'You sure do,' said Sefton, levelling the Colt at Seth Lancing's head.

'Don't shoot, mister, whoever you are. I'll come along with you quietly.'

'I'll tell you who I am – before I kill you. I'm Cal's uncle and Wilma Riley's brother. Remember her, Lancing? The one you raped and then throttled.'

'Please, mister,' Lancing gasped, in the certain knowledge that he could expect no mercy.

'That wasn't me. It was my brother. You gotta believe me.'

'It was both of you, skunk. Cal told me. He had to listen while you did it, remember?'

'But I didn't want to, mister. It was my brother. He forced me to do it. You don't know what he's like.'

'I can guess,' said Sefton. 'But it doesn't make any difference. Scum like you need to be put out of their misery before they can do any more damage to decent folks.'

He flicked back the hammer on the pistol and took careful aim as Lancing screamed one last desperate plea. This would be both an act of mercy and a public service. But, just as he had paused over Morrison's quivering carcass, Sefton thought again of what Cal had told him and remembered how his nephew had been made to suffer. That had been Seth's handiwork. As the degenerate in front of him fumbled desperately for the words – any words – that might stay the executioner's hand, Sefton lowered his Colt. For a moment there was complete silence as Seth Lancing stopped pleading in the belief that he was going to obtain mercy. Then Sefton fired two shots – into Lancing's kneecaps.

The scream of agony echoed through the gully, bouncing from one rock face to another, as Lancing writhed at Sefton's feet.

'Guess that settles our score, mister. That last one was for Cal.'

Sefton turned his back contemptuously and picked his way back into the sunlight. Westlake and some of the other men, alerted by the gunshots, came running up.

'Did you get him?' asked Westlake, anxiously eyeing Sefton's bloodstained shirt sleeve. Hank nodded and managed a slight grin through his pain.

'I'm afraid he doesn't want to come back with us, Sheriff. Isn't that too bad?'

THIRTEEN

Abe Lancing studied his glass gloomily. He was on his third whiskey, but tonight the alcohol didn't seem to be having any effect. He'd made it to Sedona Springs as the sun went down minus his horse. It had finally crumpled under him a mile or so out of town and he'd led it to a sheltered spot off the track to put it out of its misery. Then, having emptied the saddle-pouches and hefted his rifle over his shoulder, he tramped wearily into town.

He felt uneasy about this second visit. Sedona Springs was a lively enough place where strangers didn't attract too much attention, but he knew he was courting a risk in being here. For the moment, however, there was no choice. He was too exhausted to continue his journey without a rest, although he wasn't going to make the mistake of putting up at a lodging-house. Tonight it would have to be an unofficial shakedown in some barn or stable and an early ride out toward the railroad in the morning. At least money was no problem: the arithmetic had worked out in his favour at last. He swirled the dregs of his whiskey moodily round in the glass, drained it, turned round and beckoned to the bar for a refill. He wanted to drink enough to make sure it would put him to sleep however hard his bed turned out to be tonight. Maybe a fourth would do the trick. Unless they were watering the stuff, of course.

'Here's your drink, honey.'

Belle Dunnett slid a fresh glass on to the table by Lancing's elbow and studied the top of his hat.

'Anything else I can get you, mister? You look kind of lonely.'

'No harm in that,' replied Lancing without looking up.

'Sure there ain't. But there's no need for it. This a real friendly town.'

She sat down, unbidden, at a vacant chair. Even sitting level with him she didn't seem to be able to get a clear view of his face. The light, such as it was, was behind him, and he had his hat pulled down.

'Care to buy a lady a drink?'

Lancing was on the point of peremptorily rejecting the overture, but then an idea came to him. Maybe a bit of female company might be of practical value.

'All right. What'll it be?'

'Champagne.'

The reply had been instantaneous. Lancing gritted his teeth. In encounters like this Belle would be playing for the house, of course. But it didn't matter: even the most expensive drink in the saloon wouldn't make much of a dent in the $3,000 he had stuffed about his person. Suddenly the recollection of the money combined with the aroma of Belle's cheap scent made Lancing feel expansive.

'Fine by me. Make it a bottle.'

He fumbled in his pocket, produced a roll of dollar bills, and peeled off enough to cover the cost of at least a couple of bottles.

'Why, that's mighty generous of you, mister.'

Belle signalled over to the bar.

'You just come off a cattle drive, or something? It isn't usual for a girl to be treated to a whole bottle in this one-horse town.'

'Let's just say I struck it lucky.'

'OK by me.'

Belle shrugged, having learnt that in this business it didn't pay to ask too many direct questions. In any case sooner or later the truth usually came out. The champagne arrived and Belle poured herself a glass. Then they sat in silence for a few minutes. As Lancing downed his fourth glass the whiskey suddenly began to take effect. He sat back in his chair.

'You all right, mister?' Belle sounded concerned. She'd had plenty of practice with that question, and knew just how to ask it. Generally you could rely on it prompting a man to start talking about himself.

'Guess so. Just a bit tired maybe.'

'That's a pity.' She laid a sympathetic hand on his wrist. 'I mean,' she added, 'the night's kind of young.'

'Yeah. But I reckon I got enough to guarantee me some company till the small hours.' He patted his shirt pocket where another roll of bills was creating a visible bulge.

'Mister, with that much, you could guarantee yourself company for the whole night.'

'That so?'

Belle's words had suddenly put a thought in his mind. Why put up with the discomfort of a barn when he had more than enough money to buy himself privacy and pleasure all in one go? He was well off now – time to stop thinking and living like a hayseed.

'I guess I'm not experienced, ma'am. Don't seem to have much idea of what my money will buy.'

'Don't you worry, honey. Just leave it to Belle, here. I'll see you get full value. . . .'

'Still warm,' said Indian Joe.

It was the first words Sefton had heard him speak all day.

'Saddle must be worth something,' remarked Westlake. 'Mexican, judging by the fancy tooling.'

It had been their last diversion of the day and Indian Joe had had no difficulty in finding Lancing's dead horse a few minutes away from the trail. He removed his hand from the horse's neck and held up one finger.

'Only dead about an hour, eh?'

Westlake glanced up at the fading sun which was glowering red over the distant mountains.

'Guess he'll make Sedona Springs before sundown. But we won't be far behind him. Take the saddle and the pouches boys – even if they *are* empty. Kind of a shame to waste good leatherwork.'

'What are you going do when we get there, Sheriff?' asked Sefton.

'Find somewhere to get a bath, I reckon.' Westlake glanced across at Sefton's expression and smiled. 'Don't worry, son. He isn't gonna get away.'

'Seems to me he isn't doing so bad up to now,' said Sefton. 'And three thousand bucks sure makes things easier for him. Why don't we just ride in and comb the place till we find him?'

'Because it wouldn't be etiquette.'

Sefton snorted. 'Etiquette! What kind of fancy word is that, Sheriff? This isn't a coming-out ball we're attending.'

'Son, you aren't quite getting the picture. Kyle Brody's the sheriff in Sedona Springs, and yours truly has no authority there – 'cept under Kyle's say-so. So we pay him a visit first. Then, maybe, I get my bath.'

'But. . . .'

Sefton bit his tongue. He had envisaged the day ending with a glorious descent on their quarry in Sedona Springs, horses snorting and six-guns primed, but he was going to have to go along with Westlake's insistence on sticking to procedure. If you chose to ride with the law you had to put up with its delays.

'Anyways,' said Westlake, 'I don't reckon as how you're in need of too much more excitement with that arm.'

Sefton glanced down at his bloodstained shirt sleeve. Seth's buffet had clipped a neat sliver of flesh from over his left biceps and he would have an interesting scar as a permanent souvenir. They'd swabbed and bandaged the wound as best they could, and Sefton was making light of it, but Westlake's sharp professional eyes had noted that he was letting the arm hang down limply by his thigh to ride one-handed.

'Don't worry, Sheriff. The moment I catch sight of Lancing I promise you I won't be feeling a thing – and neither will he.'

The room was smaller than he'd imagined, but the bed sure looked tempting enough. Twenty dollars' worth of temptation, he wondered – even if you reckoned in the second bottle of champagne which they had brought up with them.

'Make yourself at home, mister,' said Belle, turning up the two oil lamps.

Abe Lancing lifted an edge of the face curtain at the window to peer down cautiously at the street outside. Then he perched uncertainly on the bed. He'd had no shortage of women before, but this was the first time he'd had the money to pay for his needs to be attended to in real comfort.

'There's no law against taking your hat off in a lady's bedroom.'

Belle smiled encouragingly across at him, and poured out some champagne as Lancing, somewhat reluctantly, deposited his dust-streaked hat on the counterpane. She passed him a glass, threw herself down in the single armchair by the dresser and eyed him speculatively.

'Guess we ought to drink a toast, cowboy.'

Abe shrugged. 'If you like.'

'What shall it be, then?'

'How about *absent friends?*'

'Suits me,' said Belle. 'I sure got enough of them.'

They raised their glasses. As Abe lifted his head back to drink, the light from the oil lamp caught him full face for the first time, offering Belle Dunnett the opportunity for the flash of recognition which the smoke-filled haze of the saloon downstairs had denied her.

'Somethin' botherin' you, lady?'

Abe Lancing was reclining against the bed-head, but his eyes were suddenly alert. The change in Belle's expression had been unmistakable.

'What? Oh . . . no . . . I was just wonderin' how you'd like to start.'

'No hurry, is there? We got all night to get acquainted.'

'Sure, mister. Why don't you just relax? Here. . . .'

She refilled his glass and handed it to him. As she did so he grabbed her other arm.

'Easy, mister, you just said we got all night.'

He put his glass down on the night table while holding on to her wrist. He could feel the shiver of alarm that shot through her body as he tightened his grip. Her face told him everything: she knew that she was alone in her room with a killer and that nobody would come looking for her till the morning. She tried to withdraw from his grasp, but he was too strong for her.

'What's the matter, don't ya like it rough?' he leered. His other hand reached up for her neck.

'That's enough, mister.'

The note of rising panic in her voice was clear: the whore had recognized him – no doubt about it. Cursing himself for leaving his rope with his horse, Lancing cast frantically around for an alternative means of throttling her. His belt would have to serve. He thrust her down on the bed with one hand while with the other he fumbled at his belt buckle.

But Belle was a well-built woman with reserves of strength and the experience to know how to make it count. Writhing under the weight of Abe's body she managed to bring her knee up into his groin. As he grunted and momentarily relaxed his grip on her wrist, she prised herself from underneath him, grabbed the brimming champagne glass from the table and flung its contents in his face.

As Lancing cursed she jumped off the bed, making for the door and safety. With the champagne bubbles stinging his eyes Lancing hurled himself after her blindly, catching the hem of her dress just as she reached the door.

Belle screamed, kicked at his face, wrenched the door open, and stumbled into the passage, with Lancing still desperately clutching at her dress. She managed to reach the banisters overlooking the main saloon floor.

'Help me, someone, for the love of Pete! He's killing me!'

Her shriek brought the cacophony of the saloon to a sudden silence as Belle stood above with dishevelled hair and torn dress.

'Some of you cahoots get on up here, goddam you! It's Abe Lancing and he's fixing to kill me.'

Some of the bolder spirits rushed for the stairs, but before they could reach Belle, Lancing had gained control of the situation. He grabbed Belle by her midriff with one hand and drew his Colt with the other.

'No closer, gentlemen, or the lady gets it!'

Belle screamed as she felt the muzzle of the revolver brush her temple. Lancing retreated cautiously with Belle back into the bedroom and kicked the door shut. Then he flung her, screaming hysterically, on the floor, grabbed his hat and pouch and was out of the window before she could get to her feet.

There was a sloping roof under the window which covered the wooden arcade over the boardwalk. When Lancing rolled down he could hear Belle screaming inside, and the sudden shuffling of boots as there was a stampede for the doors. He hit the ground just as the first of his pursuers burst through into the street.

'There he goes, the skunk. Don't let him get away!'

Lancing stumbled to his feet and made off into the darkness – wishing he hadn't left his rifle in Belle's bedroom. The mob from the saloon, their courage temporarily fired by liquor, was close on his heels calling for reinforcements from passers-by.

Lancing knew from his previous visit that there was a livery stable at the far end of the street and that it offered his best chance of escape if he could just have the luck to find a saddled horse there. He was desperately tired from the rigours of the day and his legs were so heavy that he had the impression of running impotently as in a nightmare. But he forced himself to keep going. It was just a hundred yards to the end of the street and there might still be hope. His lungs almost bursting, he careered at last towards the yard of Henschel's Livery Stables.

Judd Henschel had had a busy night. He had got his regular stable of horses nicely fed and bedded down and was just thinking of bolting up, when a posse of riders had come in from Three Rocks with their horses beaten up and needing stabling overnight. Not that he minded the business – that was always welcome – but he was short handed what with Joe, his stable boy, being laid up with a busted knee from trying to be too smart with a temperamental horse. He was just dealing with the last two horses when he became aware of footsteps running fast into the yard and a man panting hard for breath.

'Kind of in a hurry aren't you, mister?' said Judd.

Abe Lancing had no time for pleasantries. The shouts of the mob were getting closer by the second, and salvation – in the form of two saddled horses – seemed close at hand.

'The horse,' he croaked pointing to the animal under Henschel's hand, 'Gimme the horse!' He drew his Colt to emphasize his order.

'Now wait a minute, mister,' drawled Judd. 'You're making a big mistake. I just. . . .'

But Lancing had no time for discussion. With a spit of fire from the muzzle of his revolver he gunned down Henschel at point-blank range. He could hear the pounding of boots on gravel as his pursuers reached the entrance to the livery yard. Panting almost hysterically, he unhitched the horse, threw himself into the saddle and dug in his spurs.

As Judd Henschel had just tried to warn him, he had made a big mistake. The startled horse had only time to jump forward a couple of paces when the cinch strap, which Henschel had just started to unbuckle, came loose, and the saddle slipped to one side depositing Lancing literally at the feet of retribution.

'Don't try it, mister.'

There was a growl from the crowd as Lancing, sprawled winded in the mud, tried to reach for his six-shooter. There was an ominous click as he found himself staring up at the muzzle of a primed Winchester in the light of a dozen flaring torches.

'Just come and see what this sonofabitch done to Judd,' shouted an angry voice.

By now, the rifle muzzle was pressed against Lancing's heart.

'Wait a minute, wait a minute,' he pleaded. 'It was an accident. I didn't mean to shoot the old guy.'

'Like heck, mister. We ain't got much room in this town for vermin like you. We heard what you done to that farmer and his wife back at Three Rocks.'

The rifle muzzle was pressed even tighter against his vest.

'Please, don't shoot,' yelled Lancing desperately. 'I'll turn myself in. Take my guns, for Pete's sake.'

'No need to bother Sheriff Brody,' called someone from the back of the crowd. 'We know who we've got here, and we've just seen what he done. Let's string him up.'

There was a cheer of approval as Lancing grovelled in the dirt pleading for his life, but he was wasting his breath. Someone hauled him to his feet, stripped off his gunbelt and tied his hands behind his back. Next thing he was being hustled inside the shed where Henschel stored a selection of wagons and buggies. In the flickering glare of the torches a terrified Lancing watched a rope being thrown over a beam and a noose being fashioned at one end.

'No, please,' he screamed, 'you can't do this to me. I got my rights. There's law in this town.'

'That's right, mister,' a voice spoke in his ear, as the noose was fastened round his neck, 'and you're dealing with it now.'

They stood him atop one of the buckboards and drew the noose tight over the beam.

As Lancing made one last desperate plea for mercy the buckboard was kicked out of the way and his body sagged, dangling in an agony of suffocation, at the end of the rope. There was a sigh of satisfaction from the crowd as they elbowed each other to get a better view.

One old-timer remarked, 'I kind of like it when they don't have their legs tied. I do like to see 'em kicking. . . .'

FOURTEEN

'Son, you're sticking to me like a bee in sorghum.'

Matt Westlake looked round with mild irritation as Hank Sefton tramped resolutely behind him along the boardwalk in Sedona Springs. They had billeted their exhausted horses at the livery stables at the end of the street and the rest of the posse had been stood down to get themselves fed and watered. But despite his tiredness and the throbbing of his wounded arm, Sefton had refused to be separated from Westlake. He wanted to be around when Westlake broke the news to Brody that Abe Lancing was in town again. And he wanted to know first hand what Brody was going to do about it. So he had toted his Winchester on his shoulder and followed Westlake as he made his way down the street to Brody's office.

'Can't help it, Sheriff. I've kind of got used to your company.'

'Appreciate the compliment, Sefton, but you've done enough today. Why don't you leave it to the law?'

'I am leaving it to the law, Sheriff – but only as long as I'm sure that the law's going to take care of things properly. That's why I'm sticking to you.'

'Well, I guess there's sense in what you say. Never figured I'd be a chaperon to a cowboy, but there's a first time for everything!' Westlake clapped Sefton on the

153

shoulder, and they continued their walk in silence.

The sun had gone down long since and there was plenty of bustle in the streets. Sefton would have paused to peer in the doors of the various saloons that they passed, Lancing was almost certain to be in one of them, but Westlake was insistent on following correct procedure. He wouldn't risk any action without announcing himself to Brody first.

A pale yellow light was showing under the blind of Brody's office window when they arrived. Brody himself was reclining in his wooden armchair with his boots on his desk. Sefton wondered fleetingly whether that was how all sheriffs spent their time when they weren't actually outside exercising their functions. The tiny office was filled with a pungent aroma from the fat Cuban cigar that was clamped between Brody's lips. He tilted himself forward as Westlake and Sefton came in and extended his hand across the desk.

'Matt, this is kind of unexpected. Business or pleasure?'

'Business, I'm afraid, Kyle. We just tracked Abe Lancing into town. This here is Hank Sefton – brother of the lady the Lancings killed outside Three Rocks.'

'Howdy.'

Brody acknowledged Sefton, sat back exhaling a puff of cigar smoke towards the ceiling. He waved them to a pair of vacant chairs that were standing in front of the desk. Then he removed the cigar from his mouth.

'All right, tell me what's been happening.'

Westlake gave him a brief account of the day's events. When Westlake had finished, Brody took a moment to flick his cigar ash carefully into a nearby spittoon.

'Looks like we got some action in prospect, then.'

'The heck we have, Sheriff,' burst out Sefton, who had had increasing difficulty controlling himself during the leisurely interchange of information between the two representatives of the law. 'So what are we standing around here for, jawing?'

'Ain't no hurry, mister. He can't go anywhere. And if he's got a rifle like Matt says we've got to treat him with respect. I've been sheriff of this little community for over five years and I attribute my longevity to not rushing into things. I think we could do with some more men to start with. I like to have my victims outnumbered. Kind of makes me feel more secure. In any case, looks as though you could do with seeing a doctor.'

He gestured with his cigar towards Sefton's bloodied shirt sleeve.

'I'm all right. And I'll feel a whole lot better when we get to that rattlesnake who killed my sister.'

'Sure you will, son – and I'm real sorry about what happened. But keep your head cool. It's safer that way, believe me. All right. Here's what we'll do. . . .'

But what Brody's master plan would have been, they were never to discover, because at that moment there was a pounding of boots on the boards outside and the office door burst open.

'Sheriff, Abe Lancing just tried to kill Belle Dunnett up at the saloon. There's a lynch mob after him. You'd best come quick.'

Brody stared at the two cowhands who had rushed in with this news.

'All right boys, don't get excited. I'm a-coming.'

He heaved himself out of his chair and turned to Sefton. 'Guess you're about to get your action quicker than you thought, son.'

He stroked his chin for a moment. 'I think this job may call for a rifle, so if you'll just excuse me a moment, gentlemen. . . .'

He pulled a key from his pocket and opened a mahogany cabinet from which he extracted a well-oiled

Winchester. When he had methodically checked and re-checked the action and loaded it up he closed and locked the cabinet, nodding approvingly at Westlake and Sefton.

'Glad to see you're similarly equipped for the job, gentlemen. Shall we go?'

There was no doubt about the direction the mob was headed – their howling could be heard as soon as the three men stepped out of the office. Brody led them along as briskly as he could without actually running. There was a flare of torches at the far end of the street, and as they got closer, Sefton could see that the focus of attention was Henschel's Livery Stables. As the crowd suddenly erupted in a roar of triumph Brody at last broke into a run, with Westlake and Sefton panting at his shoulder. When they reached the stables there was enough light being cast by the torches inside to show what had happened. There, silhouetted against the creosoted clapboard walls, hung the soiled figure of Abe Lancing gyrating wildly at the end of a rope.

'Saved me a job,' muttered Brody as he thrust his way through the crowd with the other two right behind him.

'Maybe not,' said Sefton with a grimace.

He released the safety catch on his rifle and raised it to his shoulder.

'No, Hank,' protested Westlake. 'This ain't your business now, son. Leave him hang.'

But there was a deafening report as Sefton took careful aim and loosed off a shell over the heads of the crowd. The sudden silence was punctured by a sharp snap as the rope, from which Lancing hung suspended, broke in shreds, severed by the bullet that Sefton had sent slicing through it. The next moment Lancing crashed writhing in the dirt, eyes bulging and legs still kicking.

In a matter of seconds, Brody had broken through the crowd and was on his knees loosening the rope from Lancing's neck.

He looked up at Sefton as Lancing thrashed desperately from side to side trying to draw air into his tortured lungs.

'Well done, mister. I guess you saved him for the gallows.'

Sefton smiled with satisfaction. 'Yep. He's going to hang twice. First decent shot I've managed to fire since leaving Yuma. . . .'

It was late in the afternoon of the following day when Hank Sefton loped his horse into the yard of the Double L ranch. With his personal mission accomplished the journey back had seemed something of an anti-climax, even though he had every reason to feel triumphant. The shadow of the Lancings was lifted, and there was even a prospect of a share in the reward money. But now his thoughts were free to dwell on the family loss he had suffered – and which he'd scarcely had time to consider since the nightmare started.

He also had to start thinking about the future. Cal was an orphan and Sefton was his only relative. Not a completely destitute orphan, of course. Hank had managed to work that out from his earlier enquiries in Three Rocks. The Riley homestead would eventually pass to Cal without even the encumbrance of a mortgage thanks to Jess's hard work and frugality. Nevertheless the boy needed protection, and Sefton had to consider how best to provide it. His family visit had never been intended as more than a break from the routine of cattle driving and he certainly had not anticipated finding himself responsible for a younger relative. So as he dismounted from his horse and Cal came running up he greeted him almost with feelings of guilt. Cal had no such inhibitions, of course. He was so relieved to see Hank come back that he nearly flung his arms around him. Then, evidently recollecting his age, he checked himself and held out his hand.

'Welcome back, Uncle Hank. Sure am glad you made it.'

'Not half as glad as I am.'

Sefton touched his hat as Kathy and the other Ellwoods came out on the porch. He grinned and saluted them with a thumbs-up.

But Kathy looked concerned.

'What happened to your arm, Hank?'

'I lost a bit of flesh to Seth Lancing. Nothing I can't replace with a bit of home cooking.'

'Now that's something I *can* fix,' remarked Kathy.

It was Jack Ellwood who signposted a possible solution to Sefton's dilemma at the breakfast table the following morning. They were lingering over their coffee as one by one the various members of the household excused themselves and went about their duties. Cal had insisted on putting himself under Gus Donovan's orders with Tom Phillips, so they were left alone at the table.

They sat in silence for a few minutes absorbed in their own thoughts, and then Jack Ellwood cleared his throat.

'Er . . . look, Hank. You mind if I say something to you now we're alone? I've got a sort of proposition I want to put to you.'

Sefton looked surprised, but made no objection. 'Go ahead.'

'Well,' drawled Ellwood, 'it's like this. I won't beat about the bush. I don't know what plans you've got but I want to ask you whether you'd consider leasing me Jess's spread. I know it belongs to Cal really, but I guess it's you that has to deal for him. The thing is, the land butts on to mine and that'd be kind of useful for extra stock. But much more interesting is the water and timber that you've got up there. As a matter of fact, I'll tell you between ourselves that I offered to buy it outright from Jess a couple of times, but he was too smart to sell.'

Sefton raised his eyebrows, but made no immediate reply. Ellwood's unexpected suggestion had set his mind racing.

'Here's what I suggest,' Ellwood continued. 'You lease me the spread for seven years, by the end of which time Cal'll be old enough to decide for himself what he wants to do with it. We can work out a fair rent. In the meantime I'll offer him a job here as a ranch hand at the usual pay. You can see he's keen on ranching. By the end of seven years Gus Donovan'll have taught him just about everything he'll ever need to know.'

Ellwood paused and looked across at him.

'Well, say something, goddammit. It isn't a bad proposition, surely?'

'Why no, Mr Ellwood, it's a mighty handsome idea, as a matter of fact.'

Sefton sat back in his chair to consider the implications of Ellwood's suggestion. Not only did it offer Cal a fair path to the future, but it seemed to provide a solution to his own personal uncertainty. Last night he had feared that the pressures of family responsibilities would close the gates of freedom to him for a long time to come. But this would alter everything. There was still one point to settle, however.

'I think it's mighty handsome,' Sefton repeated. 'Always supposing Cal agrees, of course.'

Ellwood chuckled.

'Care to make a bet that he won't?'

Sefton shook his head. 'No thanks, sir. I'm not a betting man. That's why I've got money in the bank.'

Later that evening after supper they put the proposition to Cal. He listened gravely to what they had to say, and then had only one question.

'Does that mean I get to sleep in the bunkhouse with the others?'

'In a couple years, son,' said Ellwood. 'You're not quite old enough for that.' Then, noting the look of disappointment on the boy's face, he conceded, 'But you can always have your supper with the other hands out at the *parrilla* – starting tomorrow.'

'I think we've got a deal,' said Cal with satisfaction.